THE ROSE

THE ROSE

In spite of a humble background, a girl can dream...

Maid-of-all-work Alice Finlay is 17 when her employer dies and, seeking advice about her future, Alice goes to see Miss Lennox, her teacher at the orphanage, her former home. Alice has a talent for drawing and Miss Lennox finds her a position with Simpson's, where she is taught the art of decorating pottery. As she learns her craft, Alice becomes involved in the lives of her friends at work, and even has her own romance, but she is determined to be a 'proper artist' – a dream which is realised in the sale of her first picture, a Scottish rose.

The Rose

by

Anne Forsyth

Dales Large Print Books
Long Preston, North Yorkshire,
BD23 4ND, England.

British Library Cataloguing in Publication Data.

Forsyth, Anne
    The rose.

    A catalogue record of this book is
    available from the British Library

    ISBN   978-1-84262-719-8 pbk

First published in Great Britain in 2008 by
D C Thomson & Co. Ltd.

Cover illustration © Nigel Chamberlain by arrangement with
Alison Eldred

The moral right of the author has been asserted

Published in Large Print 2009 by arrangement with
Anne Forsyth, care of Dorian Literary Agency

Dales Large Print is an imprint of Library Magna Books Ltd.

Printed and bound in Great Britain by
T.J. (International) Ltd., Cornwall, PL28 8RW

Chapter One

All Alone

'Well, what's to be done with this lot?' Mrs Macfee glared round the room at the furniture.

Alice very nearly giggled. Suppose – just suppose – the furniture answered back. The large horse-hair stuffed sofa, the imposing sideboard, the array of china ornaments along the mantelpiece – just suppose they answered back and said, 'Leave us alone.'

Mrs Macfee adjusted her feather boa and turned her gaze on Alice, who quickly composed herself to stand meekly before her.

'And what's to be done with you?' she thought, but she didn't say it out loud.

She was a scrawny thing, all arms and legs, this Alice, who had been maid of all work to old Aunt Elsie. Strong, though. Mrs Macfee knew that. Ever since Alice had come from the orphanage at fourteen, she had worked hard for Aunt Elsie, who could be difficult.

'As I well know,' she said to herself.

Up and down stairs, answering the old lady's bell, rung at all times of day and night, cleaning out grates, and dusting all this hideous Victorian furniture – yes, Alice had worked hard.

She had been a good servant, Mrs Macfee allowed. Then she gave herself a little shake. It was time to sort things out, make plans, and then she could be off, back to Glasgow and her comfortable home in the West End, with its electric light and the newest of furniture.

'Well, now,' she said quite kindly, looking at Alice, who stood, hands folded, waiting to hear what Miss Macintosh's niece had to say.

Alice remembered the old lady with affection. Oh, she was often a trial, but kindly with it. Alice had not known much kindness and she recognised that Miss Macintosh had been good-hearted, lonely and grateful for company. And now she had gone.

'And what's going to happen to me?' Alice wondered.

Cook had already gone, some weeks ago.

'Right,' she had said. 'As soon as I've got my wages that's owed me, I'm off.' She had glanced round the old-fashioned kitchen. 'And I won't be sorry to leave this place, I can tell you.'

Alice had not liked the cook very much. She was usually ill-tempered, and had made no effort with meals, sending up unappetising dishes to the old lady. Miss Macintosh had not complained, though she would have preferred something light and tempting.

'And if you know what's good for you, my girl,' Cook had told Alice very firmly, 'you'll be off yourself. No point in hanging around. It's not as if–' and she had laughed raucously '–not as if you were going to inherit any of this.'

'I wouldn't expect to,' Alice had said stiffly.

'Ah, well.' Cook had looked at Alice with a rare expression of compassion. 'I dare say they'll find you something. I'm away to my sister in Largs. She'll need help with the boarding house. Her man's feckless – no use at all – so she'll be glad to see me.'

Alice had wondered if this was true. Somehow she did not think that Cook's sister would welcome her strident, opinionated relative. But she had said nothing.

Alice had waved goodbye as the carrier hefted Cook's trunk down the steps and on to the cart, and then she had heaved a sigh of relief. She herself had decided to stay on until Mrs Macfee arrived.

'It's not as if I have anywhere else to go,' she thought.

Mrs Macfee, when she arrived, had seemed at a loss as to what to do with Alice.

'You've been very lucky to find such a good place,' she said with a sniff, 'coming as you did from the orphanage.'

Alice was irritated by this. 'I know fine I'm an orphan,' she thought, 'but that's not my fault. Anyway, I worked hard for the old lady.'

She knew, though she would not herself have called it luck, that she was more fortunate than many of the orphans. Most of them had gone into the linoleum factory, one or two to the linen works. The matron had singled Alice out.

'You're neat, clean, lady-like,' she had said a little grudgingly. 'I think you'd suit.'

And as soon as she left school, Alice, her few possessions in an old leather bag, had been sent to the big house.

Oh, it had been lonely at first. She sometimes wished Matron *had* sent her to the linoleum factory, though she knew she would have hated the noise and the smell. But the company – oh, how she had missed the other girls: Maisie, with her defiance of Matron, and Maggie, with her fund of stories. And Alice had been sorry to leave school, though there hadn't been any question of staying on. She could read, write and count, and that was enough ... for an orphan.

But Alice had one talent that the other orphans lacked. She had known, ever since she was a small child, that she could draw. In the little spare time she had, she drew people, flowers, leaves, on any scrap of paper she could find.

At Miss Macintosh's, Alice had found she had to work hard, from the moment she rose in the morning to clean out the grates, until last thing at night when she set the tray for the old lady's breakfast. But she had had a half-day each week, and then she had escaped to the park. She'd enjoyed wandering in the sunshine, feeling the freshness of a light spring breeze. She'd been accustomed to taking with her a pencil and a sketch pad, and she would sit on a bench, drawing the pattern of sycamore leaves, or sometimes sketching people – a boy running with a hoop, a baby in a bassinet, muffled in clothes and peering crossly from beneath a frilly starched bonnet.

It had been the one way of escaping the drudgery of her daily work, and she had looked forward to those snatched few hours.

But now she wondered what was going to happen to her.

Mrs Macfee looked at her, and shook her head doubtfully.

'Well,' she said, 'we'll need to make arrangements for you.'

'Just as if I was a parcel,' Alice thought resentfully.

'The house will be sold, of course,' said Mrs Macfee. 'But you can stay on here till we get it cleared out. And then, have you thought of where you'll go? You haven't any family, even at a distance?'

Alice shook her head. 'None.'

'Ah...' Mrs Macfee felt a moment's pity, but then she was brisk again. 'It's lucky that you're in Kirkcaldy – there are plenty of jobs going in the linoleum works.'

'I don't want to go into the linoleum works.'

'Indeed?' Mrs Macfee was not prepared for this. 'And why not, may I ask? Plenty girls of your sort do.'

'I...' Alice paused. 'I don't like the smell...'

'Don't be ridiculous! You can smell the lino works all over Kirkcaldy. And what's wrong with working there? Of course, you could go into service again. You've good experience.' She was not a very attractive girl, thought Mrs Macfee. But perhaps, with a bit more flesh on her bones, she might improve.

'No,' said Alice definitely. 'I'm not going back into service.'

Mrs Macfee sighed. This was proving more difficult than she had thought.

'Well, what do you want to do then?'

'Something to do with drawing or painting,' said Alice dreamily.

Mrs Macfee sniffed. 'My dear girl, you need training for that, and who's going to pay, may I ask?' Of course, she thought with only a moment's pang of guilt, the house would fetch plenty, but then, there was her daughter, Georgie, soon to be married, and Laurence at university, and it was going to cost them a pretty penny before he graduated, if he ever did.

Of course, there would be something for Alice, a keepsake like a necklace, for example. But money – no, there wouldn't be any to spare.

There was an awkward pause.

'I'll find something,' said Alice. 'You don't need to worry about me.'

'Well,' said Mrs Macfee, who was rather relieved to hear this, 'you can stay here for the month. I'll show you what's to be done. We'll need to clear her room–' She shuddered as she thought of the old lady's bedroom, the high bed and the huge wardrobe, the tables crammed with family photographs and china, the heavy dark green brocade curtains.

'Missus...' Alice was hesitant, 'what about food and stuff?'

'Oh, you mean money? I'll take care of the tradesmen's bills–' and here she hesitated. 'And I'll give you something to be going on with.' She reached for her velvet bag and brought out her purse. 'Will that do?'

When she had given the last of her instructions, the door closed behind her, and Alice watched as she made her way into the hired car.

For a moment the girl felt slightly envious. She had never been in a car, although now, in Kirkcaldy in the early twentieth century, lots of people had them. The doctor, for example, and some of the rich people who lived near the Park.

But then she realised that she wouldn't change places with Mrs Macfee.

'She's just after what she can get,' thought

Alice sagely. 'She never came near the poor old lady when she was alive.'

But then she dismissed Mrs Macfee and it dawned on her that for the first time in her life, she was free. She danced up the stairs and jumped down two steps at a time, landing on the oak floor and sliding across until she reached the door. Then it occurred to her that this was perhaps not quite the thing to do with her employer only dead a week past. But, well, the old lady had had a sense of humour – Alice felt sure she would have understood.

She paused in front of the long mirror in the hall and glanced at her reflection. She saw a tall girl wearing a long skirt and a white blouse, covered by a drugget apron. The blouse had shrunk and clung to her thin body. Her auburn hair was tied back from her face. No-one could have called her pretty, for her features were plain, with a pointed chin, but she had wide blue eyes and a clear, open expression. She sighed as she looked in the mirror, with its spotted glass.

'I'm not likely to get a lad,' she told herself frankly. 'So I might as well get a job I'll enjoy. I'm not going to work in the mill. I'm not going to be a skivvy in someone else's house,' she repeated. She was perfectly sure of that. 'I want to work and learn, and do what I want.'

For the first time in her seventeen years, she knew that she could decide for herself. But then, suddenly disheartened, she sat down on the lowest step of the stairs. How on earth was she to begin?

Outside she could hear the rumble of carts and the tramps of hob-nailed boots. She went to the window and drew aside the net curtains. People were going home from work, shouting to one another, piece tins clanking.

She began to feel excited at the thought of being one of them, no longer shut away at the whim of an old woman, lonely, unable to make friends outside the vast Victorian villa.

'I don't know a soul I could ask for help,' she thought, suddenly despondent. And then she remembered. 'Yes, there is some-one. There *is* someone I could ask for help.'

As she sat on the lowest step of the stair-case, Alice's thoughts drifted back to those days. It all seemed a long time ago, and yet it was only four years since she had left the orphanage that had been her home for as long as she could remember.

As long as she could remember...

'She's come from a good home, you can

16

tell,' said Matron to her assistant, surveying the scrawny little figure who stood defiantly before them.

'What happened to the parents?' The assistant had lowered her voice.

'A sad case,' Matron murmured. 'The father was lost at sea, and the mother died, poor thing – tuberculosis.'

Her assistant nodded. There were very few families who escaped, families who lived in cramped, unhealthy conditions. How could they expect to bring up strong, healthy children? And this child would probably have died too, if a zealous neighbour hadn't called the authorities.

'She's a fortunate bairn,' said the assistant.

The matron nodded, but she wished Alice was more aware of her good fortune.

'She's a difficult child,' she said. 'Head-strong, determined. It's a pity she's not more like the other girls.'

Indeed, Alice was *nothing* like the other girls. It was she who had rebelled when the sewing class were making aprons of a hard, unyielding linen. What was the earthly use of adding elegant hemstitching to an apron that was to be worn when scrubbing floors?

'I'm not doing hemstitching on mine,' she told the sewing teacher.

17

'You'll do as you're told,' said Miss Ross, a grim-faced woman.

'But...'

The other orphans looked on, half of them amazed and admiring, the other half waiting to see what would happen to Alice. She was a bold one, some of them thought. It would take more than old Miss Ross to frighten her.

The teacher confronted Alice. 'I hope I did not hear you rightly. You are an impudent girl.'

'I only said...' Alice was quite prepared to argue her case.

'I know what you said.' Miss Ross's voice rose. 'Now sit down at your table and continue your work.'

'But can't you see?' Alice protested. She thought her argument was perfectly reasonable. 'It's a waste of time. We could be sewing something – well, beautiful.'

'Something beautiful...' the teacher echoed sarcastically. 'I can see there is no use arguing with you. You will go to Matron's office.'

'I don't know what is to become of you, really I don't.' Matron was exasperated by Alice's appearance. And exasperated, too, by her subordinate's lack of discipline. Why couldn't she keep control of a class? In fairness, she thought, most of the orphans were docile and well-behaved. None of the others argued as Alice did.

How dare she, this child who had been brought here as an infant, who might have died but for the neighbour's prompt action? She had a good home and would later be trained to go into service, or into the mill. She was fed and housed and educated. What more could the girl want?

'You will apologise to Miss Ross,' she said, 'and do as you are told.' She sniffed into her handkerchief and dismissed the child.

'I don't know how you dared,' Alice's friend Maisie said admiringly to her later.

'I don't care. I want to make beautiful things. I want to learn to be an artist,' said Alice firmly.

'But us orphans,' said Maisie, 'we've got to do as we're bid.'

'Not me,' said Alice, ending the discussion.

There was one glimmer of hope, something on the horizon to look forward to: the annual orphans' picnic, organised by a group of local ladies. The orphans, scrubbed and tidy, hair brushed, wearing their best starched white pinafores, were taken by charabanc to Lower Largo where they were allowed to play on the sands, run races and were given milk and buns. Or they might go inland, to a picnic in the fields around Springfield.

This time it was an outing to the country. Some of the girls murmured that they would rather have been by the sea, but Alice was in her element. As soon as they scrambled out of the coach, she set off searching for grasses and wild flowers. There was pink campion and lady's smock and wild violets and before long she had gathered a small posy.

'What are you going to do with these then?' Maisie asked her.

'I'm going to try to draw them,' said Alice.

'Huh... Come on, you'll be late for the races,' Jessie said, already running off.

The milk and buns tasted like nectar in the clean fresh air, and the good lady benefactors looked on, pleased with their efforts.

'Poor things,' said one, remembering their own children in their warm nursery. 'They have so little.'

Eventually the orphans climbed back into the charabanc chattering eagerly about the day.

Only Alice sat quietly. She had dipped her handkerchief in the burn and wrapped it round the stems of her wild flowers, willing them to last until they reached the orphanage.

Later, as she sat sketching the flowers, she wished she could paint them to try to capture their vibrant colours – the deep glowing purple of the violets, the clear pink of the campion. They didn't look as she remembered them, not when they were drawn in pencil.

'What are you doing, girl?' Miss Lennox sighed. All the other orphans in her class were docile, obedient girls. They'd chant the nine times table without a mistake, and they would recite a poem from memory without faltering; perhaps without expression or emotion, either, but you couldn't expect that, Miss Lennox told herself. It was enough to teach these children to read and write and count. Most of them would be going into the mill anyway, so what need had they of poetry?

All the same, she wondered if among these quiet well-behaved girls in their serge dresses and pinafores, there might not be one with imagination, with a spark of ambition.

And now, she recognised the girl who was concealing a piece of paper under the desk lid.

'Come here, girl,' she ordered.

Alice Finlay flushed but did not try to hide what she was doing.

'Give it here,' said Miss Lennox, taking the piece of paper.

She glanced at it. It was a sketch of marigolds in a jar on the teacher's desk. Often when she asked her class to draw a flower, she received stilted attempts, stiff stems, blooms bent at an awkward and impossible angle. But this – the marigolds were well drawn. Alice had noticed the shape of the petals, and she'd tried her hand at shading.

Miss Lennox herself was an amateur artist; she had recently had a painting hung in a local exhibition. And at that moment she recognised that this child, with her hair scraped back and her thin arms and legs, was different from the other orphans.

'You know quite well you are disobeying me,' she said sternly. 'You are supposed to be copying out the poem on the blackboard. Go back to your seat and I will speak to you at the end of the lesson.'

Alice flushed as the rest of the class giggled or sent her pitying looks.

'Well, what have you to say for yourself?' said Miss Lennox later, when Alice stood before her desk.

'My drawing wasn't very good. I can do better. It should be coloured.'

Miss Lennox was even more surprised. Here was not the penitent girl she had expected but someone who was quite confident that she had done nothing wrong, and who was prepared to discuss her work. She spoke to the teacher as if they were equals.

'You like drawing?' Miss Lennox said, deciding to abandon the lecture she had meant to give Alice.

The girl's eyes shone. 'It's what I like best. I'm going to be an artist one day.'

'Are you indeed?' She stared thoughtfully at the girl. 'Well, you'll have to work hard.'

'I don't mind.'

'And don't neglect your school work,' Miss Lennox felt impelled to add. She handed the drawing to Alice. 'You may have this back. And remember what I've said.'

'Thank you.'

Later, the girls crowded round. 'Was she angry? What did you say?'

'Not much.'

They were disappointed. She was a cool one, was Alice. Never said a great deal. You didn't know what she was thinking.

The following week, Alice was called to Matron's office. By now, this was such a common occurrence that she no longer felt apprehensive. Maybe she had lost a hair ribbon, or mislaid a book, or left some of the broth, which she hated. She had learned to close her ears to Matron's scolding.

'Come in, Alice.'

Matron looked at her disapprovingly. Thank goodness it was only a year or two until Alice left the orphanage and went into service. Then someone else would have the problem of disciplining this awkward girl who seemed to have no desire to behave like the others.

She picked up a parcel from her desk. 'This was left for you.'

'For me?' Alice stared at the parcel. She had no relatives that she knew of. She was not likely to receive a gift even on her birthday or at New Year.

'Well, aren't you going to open it?'

Hesitating, Alice undid the string and opened the brown paper.

There was a paint box, a shiny black tin, and in another twist of paper, two paint brushes.

She gazed in astonishment, and opened the tin with trembling fingers. There lay the paints, untouched – vivid blue and red and green, and brown...

'I…'

'You are a very fortunate girl.'

'But who…' Alice had a sudden thought. Perhaps this wonderful present was meant for someone else.

'Is it really for me?'

'Yes.' Matron gave a wintry smile. 'The kind giver has said you are not to know who sent it, so you will not be able to write a letter of thanks, but I think I may pass on your gratitude. You are a very lucky girl.'

'Oh, yes, thank you, thank you!' Alice's eyes shone, and Matron for once thought that there might be something in this girl after all.

'You may go…'

Clutching the precious paint box, Alice made her way back to the dormitory. All the time her heart seemed to be singing, 'I'm going to be an artist – a real artist, one day!'

Chapter Two

A Friend In Need

Alice's hands trembled as she put on her hat and checked her reflection in the mirror. She was all alone and her future was in her own hands.

'I wonder if I'm doing the right thing?' And then she gave herself a little shake. 'But if I don't, I'll only be sorry.'

There was one person she could think of to go to for help – only one.

She made her way towards the orphanage school with its high, forbidding windows. Why, she wondered, not for the first time, had they built schools like that with windows you couldn't see out of? Probably so that the scholars couldn't look out and would concentrate on their lessons. But she remembered that when she had been there she had been mesmerised by the clouds drifting in the sky above.

Preoccupied with her thoughts, Alice reached the schoolhouse door, and before she could stop to think, she had rapped on the bronze knocker. Maybe, she thought desperately, maybe Miss Lennox wouldn't be in. Maybe she had gone to visit her sister. Maybe she was asleep. No, that wasn't very likely. She couldn't picture the upright, sharp-tongued Miss Lennox ever closing her eyes, and certainly not in the middle of the day.

And then she heard footsteps, and there was Miss Lennox before her. Not very tall, but still imposing, her now greying hair swept back in a bun, wearing her Sunday best black serge with jet beading, high-buttoned black boots, and a grim expression to match. It softened slightly when she saw Alice.

'Alice Finlay!' she said. 'What do you want?'

This took Alice by surprise.

'I ... I ... didn't think you'd remember me after all this time.'

'I remember all my pupils.' Miss Lennox looked enquiringly at her, and Alice took heart from it.

'I wanted to ask you...' she began a little hesitantly.

'You'd better come in,' said her former teacher.

She showed Alice into the parlour.

'Hmm.' She looked at the girl for a moment. 'Would you like a drink of lemonade?'

'Yes ... please.'

When Miss Lennox was out of the room, Alice looked around her. A pair of china dogs ('wally dogs' she remembered they were called) by the fireplace, one on either side. Dried flowers. An array of photographs, one of a young man in uniform, staring grimly at the camera. Could this perhaps have been Miss Lennox's beau? Her fiancé, even? Maybe he had fallen in a war many hundreds of miles away.

There were shelves of books; Alice had never seen so many books. Oh, there were books at Miss Macintosh's house – but those were dusty volumes of sermons, which were never read, housed in a glass fronted case in the parlour. Here there were books everywhere, crammed into the bookshelves, piled on the table, some on the end of the sofa, and even on the floor. There was a set of Dickens' works, obviously well read, and one of Scott's; rows of poetry books, ballads, Shakespeare. And there were pictures, too. Alice rose from the horse-hair stuffed sofa for a closer look at one in particular.

It showed an Angus glen in winter, with

the snow just beginning to melt but still clinging to the black bark of the trees. Alice gazed at it, wondering why it appealed to her much more than the other pictures around the room.

'You like that one?' said Miss Lennox behind her.

'Yes, I do,' said Alice, forgetting to be abashed. 'I like it better than the others.' She glanced round at the sea scenes, the careful still life representations of fruit and flowers.

'Why?' Miss Lennox set down the tray she was carrying.

'It – it makes you shiver,' said Alice after a pause.

'Good. That's what I meant you to feel.'

'You?' Alice was puzzled. '*You* painted it?'

'Certainly,' said Miss Lennox briskly. 'Here, drink your lemonade, and have a biscuit, and then tell me why you've come.'

'It's wonderful.' Alice couldn't take her eyes off the picture.

'No, it's not,' said Miss Lennox. 'I'm only an amateur painter. But it's quite good, though I say it as shouldn't.'

There was silence for a few minutes as Alice drank the lemonade, trying to sip daintily.

'Now,' said Miss Lennox, 'tell me what you want from me.'

'I need a job,' said Alice, all in a gulp. 'Could you help me, please? I've been a maid to old Miss Macintosh but she died a few weeks ago...'

'I know.' Miss Lennox, thought Alice, would make it her business to know everything.

'You could get a job in service, or work in the mill,' said her former teacher thoughtfully.

'I don't want to work in the mill,' Alice burst out. 'And I'm tired of being in service, fetching and carrying and being shouted at.'

'Humph.' Miss Lennox reached for the poker and rattled it through the bars of the grate. A flame spurted up from the coals.

'What *do* you want to do?' she asked.

'I want to be an artist,' Alice said defiantly. 'It's the only thing I want to do. I know it costs money to train – I'm not asking for money,' she added hastily, 'but I thought you might know of somewhere ... somewhere I could maybe learn a craft.' Her voice tailed off. She suddenly felt that she had been very stupid to come here asking for advice.

Miss Lennox nodded. She had tried to

persuade the orphanage to allow Alice to stay on at school. The girl was bright, and quick to learn. And she had imagination.

'You like drawing and painting?'

Alice's eyes shone. 'Better than anything,' she said. 'Someone gave me a present when I was in the orphanage – a paint box. It meant I could paint wild flowers.' For a moment she wondered – could the mystery gift have come from Miss Lennox? But no, it wasn't possible. Miss Lennox was very fair; she wouldn't have favoured any of her pupils. And yet, Alice didn't know anyone else. Her whole life until then had been lived within the orphanage.

'A craft,' said the teacher. 'You want to learn a craft. And what makes you think you're better than anyone who works in the mill?'

Suddenly Alice flared up. 'I'm as good as anyone else. I can work and learn. Why should you say I'm not worth it?' She got up from the sofa. 'I'm sorry I came.'

There was silence, and Alice was all at once overcome with shame. Why had she spoken like that to her teacher? Miss Lennox was strict but fair, and maybe she was right. But, oh, Alice was hurt, and disappointed.

'Sit down, girl,' said Miss Lennox. 'Of course you're as good as anyone else. I just wanted to see if you had enough spirit in you. Somehow,' she said with a smile, 'I always thought you had.'

Alice stared back.

'Oh, take no notice. It's just my way.' Miss Lennox poked the fire again, more fiercely this time. 'Now, let's see what I can do to help you. Take a seat, won't you?'

Hesitantly Alice sat down again, folding her hands in her lap.

Miss Lennox reached for a biscuit and munched it, scattering crumbs over her black serge front.

'Good at art,' she said thoughtfully. 'Yes, I remember well. You had an eye for colour. Let me think for a minute…'

The room was perfectly still, except for the tapping of Miss Lennox's fingers on the arm of her chair. Alice gazed round at the pictures, at the china dogs, and the fern in the window. This plant looked as if it was tended with care; not like the aspidistra at Miss Macintosh's house, which Alice had sponged with water regularly, hating the task and wishing she could throw the plant in the rubbish bin.

'I know,' said Miss Lennox after a bit, and

Alice felt a little tremor of excitement. 'It's dull work at first, but if you're any good, you'll get a training. Have you heard of Simpson's?'

Alice shook her head.

'Well, you'll know of the Fife Pottery, where they make Wemyss Ware.'

Of course Alice had heard of the pottery; old Miss Macintosh had had several pieces – a large bowl, decorated with luxuriant pink cabbage roses; a dressing-table set painted with delicate violets.

'And there's Methven's and Simpson's,' Miss Lennox went on. 'Well, I happen to know that Simpson's are looking for staff to train... I'll have a word.'

'Oh, thank you!' Alice flushed. 'I would work hard, tell them.'

'You'd need to,' said Miss Lennox. 'I'll make enquiries and let you know. You'll have to go for an interview, mind.' She looked at the girl. Alice's Sunday coat, provided by the orphanage, was someone else's cast-off, but it was clean, and Alice herself looked fresh and neat. 'Now, where are you staying?' she went on.

'I'm still at the house till the end of the month, then I'll need to move.'

'Hm.' Miss Lennox shook her head, thinking grimly of the loyal service Alice had given the old lady, and now she was to be turned out. How could people be so uncaring?

'I wonder,' she said thoughtfully, having an idea. There was Chrissie, the woman who did her laundry. She was hard-working, outspoken, a bit of a character, but as honest as the day was long. Her husband had disappeared – no one quite knew what had happened to him – so Chrissie might well be glad of a lodger to bring in a bit extra.

'I'll have a word when Chrissie next comes to collect the laundry,' she said to herself.

'I think I can find you somewhere to stay,' she told Alice. 'Somewhere cheap. It won't be as grand as the house you're used to – it's in a poor part of the town, but–'

'That doesn't matter,' said Alice eagerly. How quickly things seemed to be moving! First, there was the chance of a job, and now perhaps somewhere to live, too.

'Give me to the end of the week. I'll talk to a few people and let you know,' Miss Lennox assured her.

Alice was aware that the visit had come to an end. She rose a little awkwardly, and tried to thank her old teacher.

'It's very good of you.'

'Don't thank me, girl,' said Miss Lennox brusquely.

She paused as she opened the door to show Alice out.

'I'm glad you liked my picture,' she said with a small, kind smile.

She stood watching as Alice made her way down the path. The girl had a spring in her step, she noted.

'That girl deserves a chance,' she told herself. 'Maybe it's not much of a start, but she's willing, and she'll learn quickly.' Her face took on a determined look that generations of her pupils would have recognised. 'She'll get her chance,' she thought, 'I'll make sure of that.'

She smiled to herself. That paint box – she had never given a gift that was more appreciated.

Alice closed the gate carefully behind her and glanced back, but the door was closed. With a heart lighter than it had been for weeks, she skipped along the road. She was going to work, and earn money and learn a craft, and make friends, and have somewhere to live. Not grand, Miss Lennox had said, but a home.

The orphanage had never been home, and she did not regard the maid's room under the eaves as homely. Oh, things looked brighter already!

'You'll be all right, lass?' The carter hefted Alice's basket over the back of the cart and set it down on the road.

'I'll manage from here,' Alice assured him.

'Right you are.' He flicked his whip and the grey cart horse set off stolidly. Alice watched until they were out of sight, then picked up her basket and looked around her.

'Coal Row,' they called it, and it certainly was dark, she thought. The houses were crammed together, so that even the bright July sun didn't seem to reach the dusty street.

She looked again at the address on the slip of paper. No. 6 Coal Row, and the name was McHarg. She wondered what her new home would be like.

'A bit of a character,' Miss Lennox had said. 'But a heart of gold. You'll be all right there.'

Alice's basket containing all her possessions was becoming heavy. There were her pinafores for work, stout woollen stockings, underwear, and her best navy blue wool dress for Sundays. Her old straw hat would have to do for now. But once she was earning – just wait!

She stopped by an outside flight of steps, and spoke to a girl who was sitting idly on the lowest step.

'I'm looking for Mrs McHarg.'

The girl jerked her thumb upwards. 'Top of the stair.'

'Are you – are you her family?'

'Me?' the girl screeched. 'Me? No, thank goodness.' She burst into peals of laughter.

Alice frowned. 'What's wrong with her?'

The girl chortled. 'She's mad, that's what.'

Just then there was a shriek from above, and a saucepan flew through the top window. While Alice jumped back, the girl looked on unmoved.

'You see?' she said. 'I told you.'

A head appeared at the top window. Alice could see a very red round face, topped by grey curls bound up in a woollen scarf.

'You nearly hit me,' said Alice, craning upwards.

'I didna mean to, lass,' said the woman. 'It was meant for our Eck but he moved.' She seemed unperturbed and was about to close the window when Alice called, 'Wait! Are you Mrs McHarg?'

'I am that,' the woman sounded suspicious. 'Who's wanting me?'

'I'm Alice Finlay.'

'Oh!' The woman leaned out, so far out that Alice thought she might overbalance. 'I thought it was tomorrow you were coming.'

'No,' said Alice very firmly. 'Today. I start work tomorrow.'

'So you do,' the woman agreed. 'Ah, well, you'd better come up. Is that your basket? Right. I'll send Eck down to bring it up.'

She slammed the window and a moment later flung it open again.

'Bring the saucepan, will you? It's a good one. I'd not like to lose it.'

Chrissie McHarg was a comfortable sort of woman. She beamed on Alice.

'Come in, lass,' she said hospitably. 'I'm just mashing the tea.'

She flung a handful of tea leaves into a pot and poured on boiling water. Alice was relieved to see that her flash of temper had apparently gone.

'You'll not mind me,' she said. 'I'm up one minute, down the next. My mother always said, "Our Chrissie should have been an opera singer." I got the temperament, right enough, but not the voice.' She chortled at her own wit, and set a couple of cups on the table.

Alice looked round the room and kitchen, at the box bed in the wall, the blazing fire, though it was a hot July day. At the rows of blue and white china on the dark wood dresser and the white anti-macassars on the two chairs by the fire. She was surprised to see that everything shone, from the brasses to the companion set in the fireplace.

Chrissie followed her gaze. 'I keep a clean house,' she said briskly. 'Miss Lennox would tell you. My mother always said, "Our Chrissie may not be a beauty but she keeps her house spotless." Now,' she went on, 'she'll have told you how I'm placed.'

Alice nodded, though in fact Miss Lennox had told her very little about her new landlady.

Chrissie went on, as she began to pour the tea, 'My man's left. I don't know where he's gone.'

'Did he not leave a note?'

Chrissie roared with laughter. 'Wouldn't have helped much, would it, seeing as I canna read or write. What do you think of that?'

Alice didn't quite know what to say, especially as Chrissie seemed quite proud of the fact.

'He'll be back one of these days,' said Chrissie comfortably. 'He'll walk in as nice as you like, expect his slippers by the fire, and a tasty piece of haddock for his tea.' She sighed nostalgically. 'He was a real handsome lad. I met him at the dancing. He led me in the Lancers. We were the best set in the hall.'

Alice had some difficulty in picturing her stout landlady as a lissom girl.

'I was real bonny then,' said Chrissie with the uncanny knack she had of divining what Alice was thinking. 'Raven tresses and a perfect complexion. And him – all the lasses were after him.'

'Would you have him back?' asked Alice.

'It depends on the mood I'm in,' said Chrissie honestly, then suddenly barked, 'See you be careful with that now!'

Alice jumped, thinking she was talking to her, but she was roaring at the boy who had entered the room, dragging Alice's basket behind him.

'This is our Eck,' said Chrissie. 'He's still at the school. But he's going into the linoleum works when he's fourteen.'

'No, I'm not,' said Eck. 'I'm going to the fishing.'

'We'll see about that,' said his mother

grimly. 'My man was at the fishing. But where he is now … I havena' seen him for years. You take that basket through to the room,' she told Eck.

'Away and unpack,' she added to Alice, 'and we'll have our tea in a wee while.'

Alice was hungry and sniffed the air appreciatively. Something smelled tasty.

'I've a nice piece of mutton, that'll do a few days,' said Chrissie. 'You'll be all right for your meat here. So, do you think you'll like the pottery?'

'I don't know,' said Alice hesitantly.

'There's some don't,' said Chrissie. 'It's too dirty for them. What did you do before, lass?'

'I was in service – to an old lady.'

'Ah, well, you'll find a difference. It'll be cheerier, that's for sure. I've got a bit of pottery – see here.' She reached up to the shelf and brought down a jug decorated with black cockerels. 'It's nice and bright, isn't it?'

'Was that made here in Kirkcaldy?'

'Aye, where else? At the Fife Pottery.'

'That's what I'll be doing, I hope,' said Alice, 'when I'm trained.'

'Aye, well, you'll get a good training at Simpson's.' Chrissie put the jug carefully

41

back on the shelf.

'Now, I'll show you where you're to sleep...'

She saw Alice look around. 'I sleep in the box bed, and Eck's round the back. You'll be through in the room.'

'The room' was bare – just a bed, and a small chest of drawers, with a swing mirror on top. A bentwood chair, and a text above the bed worked in crewel work: 'Thou, God, seest me.'

After she had unpacked and poured some water from the ewer into the basin, Alice peered out of the small window. The room looked on to a back yard, and a line of washing strung across. It was all very different from the big house near Beveridge Park. But it would be her home, and that thought warmed her heart.

Chrissie looked on approvingly as Alice cleaned her plate. 'Did she no' give you enough to eat then?'

Alice hesitated. 'The old lady?'

'Aye.'

'There was enough.' But Alice remembered how the various housekeepers who had come and gone had served frugal meals, while at the orphanage the food had been plain and dull, though there was usually enough.

Eck hardly spoke at all, except to stare at Alice and cram his mouth full of bread and margarine.

'You and me will get along fine,' said Chrissie, with a shrewd look at Alice. 'You take me as you find me.'

'I should...' Alice didn't quite know how to put it. She had no idea how much board and lodgings cost, but she had a feeling she ought to be paying much more.

'Be paying more?' Again Chrissie seemed to know what Alice was about to say. 'No, lass, that'll do me fine. I take in washing from the big houses, so a lodger will just be a bit extra.'

'But you'll let me help with the house-work.' Alice remembered that this was part of the bargain.

'There's the ironing,' said Chrissie. 'And mending. Eck's a great one for getting holes in his socks. How he does it, I don't know. You could give me a hand there.'

'I'd be pleased to.'

What Alice did not know, and what Chrissie had sworn not to divulge, was that Miss Lennox had come to an arrangement about the rent.

'I want to pay you something every month to help with Alice's rent,' she had said, looking round the kitchen, as if she could see into every corner, Chrissie had thought. 'You'll not find a cobweb here, Miss,' she had said to herself.

'Just till she gets on her feet,' Miss Lennox had said. 'I'll post the money monthly. And this is to be between us, you understand.'

Chrissie had nodded. 'My lips are sealed,' she had said dramatically.

As Miss Lennox had gone downstairs, a small group of girls, playing peevers at the end of the close, had scattered at her approach. Some of them knew her already, others recognised something in the tall, erect figure with the no-nonsense expression and knew that they shouldn't stand in her way.

'That's settled then.' Chrissie pointed towards the mending basket. 'You don't need to start tonight but there's a heap of mending just waiting there.'

After the meal was cleared away, Chrissie moved out to the flight of steps that led down to the street, and sat knitting and calling out to the passers-by. It was a sultry July evening and the sun had just reached the narrow vennel. From time to time Alice could hear shouts of laughter.

It seemed a very long evening, and Alice wished she had a friend, someone to talk to.

'Oh, stop feeling sorry for yourself,' she scolded herself briskly. At least the place was clean, and Chrissie seemed a kindly soul, and there was plenty to eat, too.

Later Alice tossed and turned in her narrow bed. Would she be able to manage the work? Was she too stupid to learn? Doubts kept crowding in, but at last she fell into an exhausted sleep.

'There you are.' Chrissie slapped down a plate of porridge in front of Alice. Eck was making patterns with milk on his porridge.

'Your first day, eh?' Chrissie said. 'Ah, well, you'll soon get the hang of it.'

Alice had taken special pains to brush her hair and tie it back, and had made sure her shoes were polished. Looking in the speckled glass, she saw the reflection of a freckle-faced girl in a dark blue dress and grey pinafore, serious but as well turned out as she could be.

As she made her way along the street she had a sudden moment of panic. All the streets looked exactly the same. Where was Simpson's? She couldn't remember...

A crowd of girls swept by, laughing and jostling, clanking their piece tins, their boots tapping on the cobbled street.

They must be going to Simpson's – or to Methven's, or maybe the Fife Pottery. Alice felt her heart thudding. What if she'd taken the wrong turning?

'Are you lost?' She heard footsteps behind her, and turned to see a girl of about her own age, her red hair covered with a scarf, carrying a piece tin, and wearing a plain grey skirt, a jersey out at the elbows, the outfit covered by a drugget apron. She peered at Alice, and said again, 'Are you lost?'

'I'm looking for Simpson's.'

'Oh, I'm going that way myself, but hurry – they ring the bell at the gate when it's clocking-in time, and if you're late...' The girl laughed, but she didn't seem too cast down by the prospect of being late for work.

With a great sigh of relief, Alice discovered that the pottery was just around the corner. Now she recognised the big iron gates. There seemed to be hundreds of people streaming in.

'What's your name? You must be new,' said her rescuer.

'Alice. Alice Finlay.'

'I'm Bet. Bet Gibson. So where are you working?'

'Just in the shed.'

'It's not bad,' said Bet. 'There's a lot of us girls. We have a laugh. But you'll have to mind out for Mr McCracken – he's the overseer.'

'I won't be scared.' Having got this far, Alice wasn't going to be intimidated.

'Maybe you won't.' Bet gave her a sharp glance. 'Come on, I'll take you in.'

'What a lot of people!' Alice was almost pushed over in the rush of people who managed to get through the gate just as the bell rang. 'Are they all workers?'

'Aye. There's the throwers and the turners, and the handlers, and the glazers and the lads in the warehouse – oh, and the painters, but they're posh, a bit grander than us. Hurry,' she added, 'or we'll be late, and Old Frosty will be wild.'

'Old Frosty? Is he the overseer?'

'Mr McCracken – that's his Sunday name. See you don't call him Old Frosty to his face!'

Alice shivered a little as they made their way from the bright early morning light into the chill of the shed. There were already small groups of girls there, chattering, some sitting on high stools in front of the pottery they were decorating. On long tables down the side of the shed were stacked white plates and bowls and cups.

Flecks of dust flickered in the shaft of sunlight that darted through the high windows.

At the far end of the shed was a large man in a white apron, wearing a flat cap. He had a florid complexion and a neat walrus moustache, and Alice recognised him as Mr McCracken – she'd met him briefly when she'd been interviewed that day in the foreman's office.

'Old Frosty,' whispered Bet. 'You'd better not get on the wrong side of him.'

He had spotted Alice and Bet. 'Ah, the new lass,' he said. 'I'm glad you're on time. Ever worked in a pottery before?' Alice shook her head.

'Well, don't go getting any fancy ideas. It's hard work. And dirty. But you've no complaints, have you?' He wheeled round on Bet.

'No, sir.' Bet kept her eyes on the ground but Alice had the feeling she was trying not to laugh.

'Now, the hours you know: eight o'clock sharp, you get half an hour for your dinner, and a break in the middle of the morning.

You get your pay on a Friday – collect it from the office. Take the seat next to Bet here.'

Alice sat down in front of a tall stand with a circular top.

'I'll start you on an easy one,' said the overseer. He picked out a white china bowl and turned it upside down on the stand.

'This is sponge painting – see?' He picked up a piece of sponge and showed Alice how it was cut into a diamond pattern. 'There's your tray of paint. Now, you dip the sponge into the paint – like this – and press it on to the bowl. You've got the rim of the bowl to keep you straight.' He demonstrated a couple of diamonds. 'See you don't smudge it. Any questions?'

There were plenty of questions Alice wanted to ask, such as, 'How many are you supposed to do?' and, 'What happens when you've finished a bowl?' She would have liked to know more about the process.

'Keep the pattern even,' he said. 'Diamonds are easy. Wait till you get on to something fancy, like a curly pattern.' He sniffed. 'Then we'll see how good you are.'

Another man in a potter's apron had appeared at the doorway.

'I'll be right with you,' said the overseer. 'And don't break any pots,' he called over his shoulder to Alice as he moved off.

Alice gulped. Very carefully, she dipped the sponge in the tray of red paint, and tentatively pressed it to the rim of the bowl.

'Press quite hard,' Bet advised. 'You can't do some light and some dark.'

The first one was the hardest. But the second was easier, and before too long Alice had completed four or five diamond shapes, all more or less evenly spaced.

Bet rose and came to inspect the work. 'That's not bad. Keep going.'

From time to time, Alice raised her head from her work to look round at the other girls. They were all about her age; some of them looked poor and shabby, and one in particular, with red-gold hair, who couldn't have been more than fifteen, was like a wraith.

It seemed as if she had been there for a whole day and she was surprised when it was only break time.

A group of them crowded together at the end of the room.

'In winter, there's a stove,' Bet explained. 'You can warm your hands.'

'This is Alice,' Bet told the other girls. 'Here, you can share my tin.' She filled a tin mug with water from the tap at the end and handed it to Alice who drank gratefully.

'So why do you want to work here then?' A big girl with a plait of hair hanging down her back planted herself on the bench beside Alice.

Alice quickly swallowed a piece of the oatcake that Chrissie had given her.

'I want to learn a craft.'

'Learn a craft?' The girl hooted with laughter. 'That's rich, that is. You'll no' learn much here, that's for sure. Fancy yourself as a lady painter, do you?'

'Oh, Jess, leave her alone,' said Bet, coming back from the tap. 'It's her first day.'

'Best she should know what it's like then,' said Jess, screwing up her face. 'It's dull work here and Old Frosty, he'll not let you get above yourself. Sponge painting's boring, but maybe you'd like to be a handler. That's great, that is – sticking handles on brown teapots all day.'

The pale, thin girl that Alice had noticed came forward shyly.

'It's nice here.' She began coughing, and Bet refilled the tin and handed it to her.

'Go on, Nannie,' she said kindly. 'Take a drink of water. It's this dust. It gets everywhere. Then it's time we were back at work,' she said, getting up. 'Here–' she gave Alice a twist of brown paper.

'What's that for?'

'To wrap round your finger when you're spinning the wheel, else your finger will soon get sore.'

Alice smiled gratefully.

She noticed that Bet went over to the next stand and spoke to Nannie, but ignored Jess. Most of the girls seemed to do that. Jess had a sharp tongue, Alice had realised already. But the rest of the girls appeared friendly enough.

She began to concentrate again, laboriously placing the sponge pattern as evenly as she could around the edge of each bowl.

She reached for another bowl and placed it on the stand in front of her. Oh, it wasn't so difficult after all, she decided, and twirled the bowl round. But she pushed it harder than she meant to, and to her horror, she knocked it from the stand. It crashed to the floor and shattered into a dozen pieces.

'Oh no!' She leapt up, dismayed. 'Look what I've done!'

She could feel pitying eyes upon her and heard Jess's sharp intake of breath.

'Here, don't get upset,' Bet consoled her. 'We've all broken pots, and it's your first day after all.' She knelt down and scooped the pieces into her apron.

'What's that? We don't pay you lasses to sit idle.' It was Mr McCracken, standing in the doorway, his eyes raking the room. Slowly he made his way down the shed, stopping at Bet's stand. She did not try to hide the pieces she had scooped up into her apron.

'Sorry, sir,' she said quickly. 'I broke a bowl.'

He shook his head. 'You broke a plate last week,' he said sternly. 'It's not good enough. Any more, and I'll stop it out of your wages.'

Alice was appalled. She couldn't let Bet take the blame. 'But...'

Bet silenced her, subtly shaking her head.

'It was me...' Alice said clearly, but one of the glaziers appeared at the door and the overseer had moved on.

Alice spun round. 'I can't let you take the blame for me!'

Bet laughed. 'Why no'? I'm used to him shouting at me, crabby old misery. I wouldn't like to be his wife. Or his son,' she added as an afterthought. 'Though his son's a good-looking lad. I could fancy him. But imagine having Old Frosty as your father-in-law.' She broke into a squeal of laughter.

'Anyway, don't worry about it,' she said.

'It's your first day. And it's only white china, after all,' she said. 'Some of the Wemyss pottery from Heron's – the broken bits end on the dump. The bairns play shops with them…'

'My auntie's at Heron's,' said another of the girls. 'The hawkers come round with their baskets for seconds and sell them in the market.'

'I wouldn't mind some of that for my wedding china,' said Bet dreamily.

'You and your wedding,' another girl scoffed.

Bet paid no attention. 'I'm going to wear white satin and have a bouquet of carnations and maidenhair fern. And white satin slippers,' she added.

'You'd better get your man first,' said Jess scornfully.

Bet laughed. 'And how do you know I've not got a lad?'

And so the chatter went on as they worked away.

When the bell went for stopping time, the girls jostled one another to be first out of the door, though Bet and Alice dawdled behind the others.

'D'you think you'll like it?' said Bet.

'I don't know,' said Alice honestly. It had

all been such a jumble of impressions.

'You don't want to pay much attention to Jess,' Bet told her. 'She's a nasty one that. Sleekit...'

Alice knew just what that meant. Sly, not to be trusted – and she had already worked that out.

But Bet, she was different altogether. Alice felt she had made a friend.

'See you tomorrow,' said Bet.

'Thanks for helping me about the bowl.'

'That's nothing.' Bet gave a cheery wave and disappeared round the corner of the street.

It had not been a bad day. Not at all. But, Alice wondered, would she ever be good enough to be a real decorator?

Chapter Three

A Grand Day Out

It was six weeks now since she'd started at Simpson's, and gradually Alice was feeling less strange. She chewed her pen holder as she sat at the kitchen table, writing a letter to Miss Lennox.

I am learning a great deal and find it all most interesting, she wrote.

Alice glanced up as Chrissie began folding the sheets she had brought home from the washhouse.

'My, it's grand to be able to write a letter,' said Chrissie admiringly. 'My mother always said I had no brains but I could take in washing, and she was right. I'll away with these sheets round to the Pottery House, and leave you to your writing.'

Having friends like Chrissie and Bet had made all the difference to Alice so that she felt less alone.

'Where would I have been without Bet?' she thought – Bet and her cheerful tones, her stories about the fisher lads she knew.

'I didna like the smell of fish at first,' she'd told Alice, 'but you get used to it.' She and Bet laughed a lot together, and on their afternoon off would wander up the High Street, admiring the magnificent hats in the shop windows, trimmed with flowers and feathers.

'I'd fair like one of those,' Bet had said.

I have made a good friend, Alice wrote, *who helped me a great deal in those first days. And Mr McCracken says I am getting more skilled.*

A week ago, he had paused by her stand

and watched as she deftly applied a pattern of flowers to the rim of a plate, placing the sponge neatly at intervals. She had been aware of him watching closely, but had kept her eyes steadily on the plate.

'Humph,' he had grunted as he moved away, 'not bad. You're learning.'

'That's high praise from him,' Bet had whispered. 'He never says that unless he's really pleased with your work.'

We're to have a works outing, she wrote, *when we go by charabanc to St Andrews. The whole works closes early for the day.*

The girls in the shed had talked of nothing else for weeks. Jess had her eye on a young man in the glazing department.

'He spoke to me this morning,' she said proudly.

The girls were supposed to carry their own boards of finished pottery to the glazing department, but now and then one of the men would take pity on a girl and give her a hand with the load, and this is how Jess had had a chance to speak to the subject of her admiration.

There had been much muttering about this. 'Why's he helping her? Her board's no heavier than the rest.'

Jess, delighted to be singled out, had

beamed on the young man. He was thin and tongue-tied but clearly attracted to her, and not at all put out by the way she ordered him about.

'He's asked me to sit with him in the charabanc,' Jess told the other girls.

Bet sniffed. 'He'll maybe have had enough of her by the time we get to St Andrews.'

Three charabancs would leave the works at eight on the Saturday morning. They were to stop at Lower Largo, and there would be time for a walk on the beach, and lemonade and buns, before the coaches set off again for St Andrews.

'We get our dinner there,' Nannie told Alice. 'And our tea at Cupar on the way back.'

Alice looked at the girl's thin frame and wondered, not for the first time, if Nannie got enough to eat.

'It sounds a great day out,' she said. 'How much–' she hesitated '–does it cost?'

Bet laughed. 'It's free. D'you think we could afford to go for a grand day out like that? No the boss pays – Mr Simpson.'

Alice had once glimpsed Mr Simpson in the outer office, in his frock coat and high collar, and gold watch chain over his stomach.

'It's real kind of him,' said one of the girls and the others agreed.

'But we work hard,' said Alice thoughtfully. 'And this is a busy pottery. He won't be short of a few bawbees. Why shouldn't he give us an outing?'

Alice!' Katie, usually silent, gazed in astonishment at Alice. 'You'll have us all out on strike. You're not one of these suffragettes, are you?'

'Not yet,' said Alice. 'But I might be. I'm only saying that we don't have to get down and grovel just because the boss gives us a day out. We've earned it.'

There was a silence. Bet broke it by saying, 'Well, I'm going to enjoy the day and never mind who's paying.'

They started talking about what to wear then. Jess had a new green wool jacket and skirt, and a white blouse trimmed with lace.

'I want to look my best,' she said, and the other girls made faces behind her back.

It was a cool morning but promised sunshine later, when the whole of Simpson's piled into the charabancs. Jess grabbed a seat by the window and pulled her young man down beside her.

Bet nudged Alice. 'He's got no chance,'

she said with a grin as she watched them.

Mr Simpson was there with his wife to see them off. He took off his hat and waved as the charabanc set off, and his wife nodded beneath her dark blue plumed hat.

Mr McCracken sat at the back of the charabanc, looking quite benign and almost unrecognisable in his best grey suit, shirt with its high wing collar, and soft trilby hat.

It was a day to remember. The drive through the quiet little coastal villages of Lundin Links and Lower Largo, then breasting the top of the hill and looking down to the broad sweep of the bay, the West Sands and the view towards the coast of Angus.

When they reached St Andrews, the charabanc stopped at the Queen's Café on the Links. Walter, who was in charge of appointments, waved a hand for silence.

'You're to be back here for your dinner sharp at one o'clock,' he told them. 'Anyone that's late we'll have eaten your share.' There was a roar from some of the potters, and a good deal of banter, before everyone scattered in different directions.

'I'm going to the shops,' said Jess. 'It's not far to Market Street.'

'Come on,' said Bet to Alice, 'let's go to

the beach.'

Alice raced after her down the embankment and on to the sands. She paused only to sniff the sea air and look out over the sea.

'Look!' she called to Bet. 'Just see how it's sparkling – like a picture.'

'You and your pictures!' Bet paused for a moment. 'Ooh–' She felt the sand damp beneath her boots, and skipped along. 'See – there's my footprint.'

'And mine!' Alice danced along beside her.

'I'm going to paddle.' Bet sat down on the sand and pulled off her black woollen stockings. 'Come on, there's no one to see us!'

Alice followed her friend.

'Oh, it's icy cold!' She could hardly remember when she'd last been in the sea – once, many years ago, when the orphanage had gone on a trip to Elie. They'd eaten ices and had been allowed to have a ride on the donkeys. Then they'd had races on the sands. She had always remembered that day.

She turned and looked back towards the town, at the grey stone houses, the sweep of the golf course, the tower of the university chapel. She wondered how it would look in a hundred years. Just the same, probably, she thought.

And then there were shouts and a group of young men ran along the sands. Two of them splashed through the shallows, pushing and jostling each other.

Alice drew back quickly, but it was too late – the runners had run by her and a spray of water splashed her dress. The young men ran on, seemingly quite oblivious. But another, who was following slowly some way behind, paused.

'I'm sorry. Did they splash you?' He pulled out a spotless white handkerchief. 'Could you use this?'

'Thank you. I didn't really get wet.' But Alice took the handkerchief and dabbed at her skirt. 'It will soon dry in the sun.'

'Are you on the trip?' he asked.

'From Simpson's?' Alice nodded.

'We're in the shed,' Bet added.

'I'm in the cashier's office,' said the young man.

'A bit grander than us.' Bet laughed. 'You don't mix with the likes of us.'

He smiled politely, and moved away.

'Come on,' said Bet. 'Stop gazing at him.'

'I wasn't!' Alice protested.

'I'm starving,' said Bet cheerfully. 'It's the sea air. Soon be time for our dinner.'

The girls strolled up the embankment and

Alice's eye was caught by a poster.

'Oh, wouldn't that be grand – look, it's Sanger's Circus. There are sea lions, and a thought-reading pony. I wonder how they teach it to read people's minds?'

'Don't be so daft. It's a trick!' Bet scoffed, and the girls argued amiably on this topic for a moment or two.

'Forget it,' Alice finally said, laughing. 'We won't be here anyway. Let's have a quick look at the shops.'

The other girls had been shopping, too. Nannie was clutching a bag of sweets to take home. Jess had been window-shopping, dragging her young man along.

'Oh, you should see the Peter Pan collars. I'd like one of those. And the trussore silk blouses.'

As they sat down to the meal, Alice found herself sitting a few seats away from the young man they had seen on the shore.

She bent her head over her plate. He was, she thought, quite good-looking – dark hair sleeked back, dark eyes. Rather pale, perhaps, but that was maybe the result of having an indoor job.

After the waitresses had poured tea from huge teapots, people began to plan how they'd spend the afternoon. To her astonishment, Alice turned round and found the young man at her elbow.

'I'm George Jamieson,' he said. 'And you are?' he asked politely.

'Alice Finlay.'

'Perhaps Miss Finlay, I could make up for this morning,' he said.

'There's no need. It wasn't your fault.'

'Maybe you and your friend,' he nodded at Bet, 'would like to come and watch the Pierrots this afternoon? I'm told they're very good.'

'I've never seen a Pierrot show,' said Bet eagerly.

'Then now's your chance. Willie's Pierrots are the best,' he said.

'All right then,' Alice agreed shyly.

It was indeed a splendid show, and afterwards, as they strolled back, Alice thought how changed people were when they were on a day off. Even Mr McCracken, waiting beside the charabanc, looked quite different in his best suit instead of the flat cap and apron.

'Enjoying the day, are you, lassies?' he said with a smile.

'It's wonderful.'

'Aye, grand weather. They say it's going to be the hottest summer ever.'

'You've not been to see the Pierrots, Mr McCracken?' Bet asked cheekily.

'Me? Oh, no, I've no time for such like frivolity, not when there's the Castle to see, and the Cathedral. Full of history, St Andrews. The very stones... And we've little enough time.'

Bet giggled while Alice, turning round, caught George's eye and blushed.

'Don't be so silly,' she told herself firmly.

'I couldn't eat another thing,' Nannie said wistfully. 'I wish I could take some of this home.'

'Aye, it's been a grand tea,' one of the men from the glazing department agreed, opening the buttons on his waistcoat as if to prove the point.

'A fine day altogether,' Mr McCracken pronounced.

Before they rejoined the charabanc, Walter called for three hearty cheers for Mr Simpson. Alice joined in rather absently. She was conscious of George standing beside her and of his glance resting on her every time she turned round.

'You've got yourself an admirer,' Bet whispered, as they took their places on the charabanc.

'Oh, nonsense. Away with you.'

But that evening Alice was a little quiet as images of the dark-eyed young man stayed with her.

Chrissie wanted to know all about the day, though, roaring with laughter when Alice described the Pierrots, asking what the other girls had worn, and cupping her hands round the little china ornament that Alice had brought her.

'Och, lassie, you shouldn't have,' she said, but Alice noticed that she put it carefully on the mantelpiece between the mug inscribed *A present from Rothesay* and the Coronation mug that young Eck, along with all the other schoolchildren, had been given last month.

Alice didn't mention George. Somehow, she didn't want Chrissie to know about him. And after all, she wasn't likely to have anything more to do with him – was she?

After the outing, things seemed rather quiet. Once the girls had gone over and over the events of the day, there seemed little else to say.

It was, as they'd been promised, one of the hottest summers ever, and at break times some of the girls would wander outside to soak up the sun. Others were glad of the cooler atmosphere inside the shed and thankfully gulped down mugs of water.

'Have you seen that lad again?' Bet wanted to know.

'Which one?' Alice was off-hand.

'You know fine. The one in the cashier's office.'

'Oh, him.'

'He could be a catch, that one.'

Alice shook her head and got up to fetch a mug of water, pushing her hair back from her brow. Even here indoors, it was hot and sticky, she felt her blouse clinging to her shoulders.

She glanced round the group, and felt for the piece of paper and the pencil in her overall pocket, a comforting presence that took her mind off the boredom and heat and a vague sense of unease, too. Did it have to do with George, she wondered? How pleasant he was. How polite. He seemed different from the lads in the glazing department. Was he really interested in her?

But then she told herself firmly, 'You're as bad as Bet.'

Sitting a little way apart from the group, she listened with half an ear to Jess and Bet arguing, Jess's sharp tones clearer than the other voices. She noticed Nannie, hunched over her mug of water and an unappetising hunk of bread.

Quickly, Alice began to sketch. None of the others paid any attention to her.

'Come on,' said one girl, putting down her piece tin. 'That's the break over.' She yawned. 'I wish it was stopping time.'

'What's that?' Suddenly Jess was peering over Alice's shoulder. Alice tried to hide her drawing, but Jess snatched it out of her hand.

'See this!' she called to the others. 'The new lassie's drawing.'

'Let's see!' They all crowded round.

Jess smoothed out the paper.

'It's Nannie!' said Bet.

'It's really like her,' said another admiringly. 'You've got the hair and the face. It's Nannie, as clear as anything.'

Nannie gazed at her picture. 'No one's ever done a drawing of me,' she said. 'Could I – could I take it home to show my mother?'

'It's not that good,' Alice apologised. 'I could do a better one if I had time.'

'What's this?' It was the overseer. Nannie hastily put the drawing in her pocket. 'You're not paid to sit around gossiping, you lassies.'

After that, when the girls gathered round

at a dinner break, there would now be a clamour for Alice to produce sketches, so that from being the new girl, the outsider, she gradually became one of the group. She would pull out a scrap of paper from her pocket, and with swift confident strokes would sketch a likeness. There was Jess – she was not too pleased with the drawing Alice did, but the others recognised the sharp black eyes, the watchful mouth.

'It's no' like me,' she protested. 'I'm a lot bonnier than that!'

There was Bet, her curls escaping out of the band around her head, her face alert and lively. And the others – some were harder to draw than others, but Alice enjoyed the challenge.

There was one day when Alice, waiting for a new batch of pots to arrive, watched Mr McCracken closely. The flat cap, the apron, tied firmly around his waist, the long pale face with the walrus moustache. She had a good visual memory, she knew, and as soon as he had gone, she made a quick drawing of him.

'It's just like him,' Bet giggled, looking over Alice's shoulder.

'Let's see! Let's see!'

'Ssh … he's coming back.'

But it was only a lad carrying another batch of pots on a large wooden tray.

'More work for you lasses,' he said. 'Now you canna stand about blethering.'

Alice hastily stuffed the drawing under a plate. It was one of the best she had done, she knew, and captured exactly the overseer's grim expression.

She was working on an especially detailed pattern and needed all her concentration, and she quite forgot about the drawing.

It wasn't until much later that she remembered.

'I've got a nice piece of herring for your tea,' Chrissie had said. 'Done in oatmeal, real tasty.'

Alice was enjoying it until she remembered. She suddenly laid down her knife and fork.

'What's the matter, lass?' Chrissie's sharp eyes missed very little.

'Nothing,' Alice gulped. But, of course, there was.

She had left the sketch of Old Frosty on her stand. He would be in first thing, checking the supply of pots. He was sure to see it, wasn't he?

Alice felt a lurch of panic. She no longer had an appetite. She swallowed with difficulty and took a gulp of tea.

He would see it. And he would be furious. Quite right, too, for it wasn't a very flattering sketch.

Worse still, he might be offended. Alice did not particularly like the overseer; he was old and grumpy, and she had never seen him smile, except for the day of the outing. But for all that, he was fair. He'd never actually praised her work, but now and then there was a grudging 'Not bad,' and she knew that was the best she could expect.

At the same time, Alice would never have wounded him. She imagined him finding the sketch. How awful for a proud man! Maybe he would be badly hurt; maybe he would take it home, but wouldn't show it to his wife, or to his son, that lad he was so proud of that had gone on to take all the prizes at school and was now a student at the university.

'Oh, how could I?' Alice thought. 'How could I be so stupid!'

'Here, lass, eat your tea.' Chrissie was concerned.

'I'm sorry. It's just – I'm not very hungry.' Alice got up and rushed from the table, leaving Chrissie staring after her in dismay.

All night long, Alice tossed and turned.

She lay sleepless until the first light trickled through the thin curtains.

'You're being ridiculous,' said Bet bracingly. They had met as usual at the corner of the street on the way to work and immediately Alice had poured out her worries. 'Anyway, what does it matter?'

Alice stared at her. 'Of course it matters!' And as she spoke, she remembered Miss Lennox saying, 'You will take life hard. You will fret over trifles, build mountains out of molehills.'

'Of course it matters,' she said again. This was not a trifle, she thought. It was something important.

'Maybe it'll still be there,' said Bet, trying to comfort her.

'Maybe,' she agreed doubtfully.

Alice reached her stand. She closed her eyes and prayed to the God who in Sunday School had seemed such a stern, remote figure, like a teacher who awarded good and bad marks. But now she needed help.

'Please, please, let him not have found it,' she begged.

But the paper had gone.

Chapter Four

Poor Nannie

'Should you be at work?' Alice looked anxiously at Nannie as she tried to catch her breath after another bout of coughing.

'I'm fine.' Nannie looked up at Alice, who noticed that the younger girl's face was flushed. She seemed thinner than ever. 'It's just the dust.'

Alice said nothing more. Nannie had been like this all winter. Now it would soon be spring and the doors of the work shed stood open to let in the sunlight. Alice had recently been promoted to transfer painting, and now she worked at the far end of the shed.

'You'll no' find this as easy,' the overseer had told her.

But Alice was determined that he shouldn't have cause to complain. She worked slowly and meticulously, placing the transfers with care. And now and then he would nod as he passed. 'Not bad.'

She tried hard not to worry about whether he had found the sketch she'd done. But, she reasoned, there was nothing she could do about it, except work so hard that he couldn't help having a good opinion of her, and see her as steady and responsible.

Alice had been afraid that her promotion would mean her companions in the shed would be envious, maybe a little jealous. But still she gathered with the other girls at break time.

Other girls, such as Jess, who had worked at the pottery for years, seemed to work at sponge painting as if they were machines. Why had none of them wanted to try for promotion, she wondered. She put this to Bet one day.

Bet gave her usual hearty laugh. 'Me, I'm not wanting to move anywhere. I'm fine where I am. Until I get married,' she added, and laughed again.

Alice thought a lot about Nannie, patient, uncomplaining Nannie. No-one seemed to know very much about her or her family. She worked slowly but carefully, printing regular patterns, and never seeming to weary.

'She's not very well,' Alice said in an aside, as they stopped for the mid-morning break.

Bet glanced over at Nannie. 'You'll not get her to stop.'

'It's not good for her, all this dust,' said Alice indignantly. 'She shouldn't be working here.'

Bet made a face. 'And where else would she work? There's the linoleum factory – and that's harder than here. Or the linen mill.' She shook her head. 'There's nothing much we can do about it.'

When Alice returned to her own place, she picked up the bowl on which she was working and tried hard to concentrate on her work. It was all too easy to spoil a pattern or even break a piece of pottery if your mind was elsewhere.

At home time, as she crossed the yard, someone stepped in her path.

'You'll not remember me,' said the young man, smiling at her. 'From the outing, George Jamieson – remember?'

Alice blushed, feeling a little confused. 'Oh, yes,' she said.

'Are you on your way home?'

'Well, yes...' Bet was meeting a lad that evening and had hurried away as soon as the bell rang.

'Then I'll walk with you part of the way, if you've no objection.'

How polite he was, Alice thought. Not that she was a snob, but it was nice to meet someone with good manners, like the smooth, elegant young men in the magazines that the girls passed around.

'I live in Coal Row,' she told him.

'I'm not sure I know where that is,' he said.

'There's no need to come all the way.' Alice didn't want Chrissie watching from the window and making comments about her escort.

'Very well.'

Conversation was a little stilted as they walked along. Alice was only too conscious of her grubby pinafore, the dust in her hair. By contrast, George looked smart and his white collar was still spotless.

'Have you worked at Simpson's long?' she asked.

'Ever since I left school,' said George. 'I learned book keeping at evening classes. In fact, I'm still at night school, one evening a week. It's the way to get on.'

'Oh yes,' said Alice eagerly. 'I want to get on, too. I'd like to be a decorator.'

He smiled down at her. 'I'm sure you're good enough.'

They were silent then. He put his hand

under her arm, protecting her when a message boy on a bicycle swerved too near the kerb, or when a horse and cart clopped past. She liked the way he walked on the outside of the pavement, like a real gentleman – 'I must remember to tell Bet,' she thought.

When they parted at the corner of the street, he said, 'I go this way,' and then paused, before rushing on, 'I wonder – would you like to come for a walk in the park some time?'

'I'd like that,' Alice said, blushing.

'We could maybe go and listen to the band. Say Saturday afternoon?'

They arranged a meeting place, he raised his hat, and Alice watched him as he walked away.

'I'm going out this afternoon,' said Alice when she returned to her lodgings at Saturday mid-day.

'With a lad?' Chrissie was curious. 'Are you walking out then?'

Alice blushed. 'Oh, no, nothing like that. It's just someone from the works...'

'You're young yet.' Chrissie looked at Alice with a speculative eye. 'But none the worse for that. If you're a wise-like lassie, you won't let him take liberties with you.'

'Oh, no, of course not,' said Alice hastily. 'I hardly know him.'

Chrissie shook her head. 'My Johnnie wasna' easy scared off. He was determined to have me. And after a bit, we got wed. We had to, with a bairn on the way,' she said frankly. 'I'd have done better to listen to my mother. I was too young to get married. Mind you, Johnnie's a good man – when he's here.'

'Do you not know where he is?'

'I've no idea,' Chrissie said cheerfully. 'But then, there wouldn't be any use him sending a postcard wi' me not able to read.' She started folding towels neatly. 'He'll turn up one of these days.'

The outing with George was one of the most pleasant days Alice could remember.

'Let's forget about work for today,' he said when they met. 'May I say how attractive you look?'

Alice blushed. She was wearing her best skirt, and a crisp white blouse buttoned to the neck, with her hair tucked up under the straw hat she had trimmed with artificial daisies.

'Now,' he suggested, 'why don't we listen to the band for a bit, then have tea – or ices, if you'd rather?'

'That would be fine.' Alice sparkled up at him and he thought how pretty she was, this girl with her wholesome pink and white complexion and strands of auburn curls escaping from under her hat.

'Then that's what we'll do.'

The afternoon went by too quickly for them both.

'Let's go for a walk some other day,' he said as they said goodbye. 'I've enjoyed this – have you?' he asked almost anxiously.

'Oh, yes…' It was a new experience for Alice, and she hugged to herself the memories of the afternoon – the sunshine, his hand under her arm, the ice-cream and tea, and the dainty cakes. It was a whole world away from the one she knew.

'Fancy – me, an orphan,' she thought, 'with a young man.' Not that he *was* her young man, not yet, but you never knew…

A few days later, Alice was struck again by Nannie's appearance. Maybe Chrissie would know something about her and her family.

'There's a girl at work – Nannie Macfarlane. Do you know anything about her, or where she stays?'

'Fine I do,' said Chrissie. 'They live up

Nicol Street.'

Alice nodded. She knew Nicol Street, a narrow row of three-storey houses, houses with small windows. Families lived close together. She'd seen some of the children running about. They looked poor and shabby, though they didn't seem to be miserable, and shouted raucously to one another as they kicked an old tin can up the street. Sometimes the girls had found an old bit of rope and played skipping games in the street.

'They're poor folk, Nannie and her mother,' said Chrissie with a sigh.

'Nannie's not well.'

'No.' Chrissie shook her head. 'She'll go the same way as her sister. The mother's a feckless body. It's Nannie has to keep that place going.'

'It's the dust in the shed,' Alice persisted. 'No wonder she's always coughing.'

'Nothing you can do about it, lass. She's lucky to have a job and a wage coming in regular.'

During the next few days, Alice kept a watchful eye on Nannie, and she and Bet took turns in finishing off a bowl whenever Nannie's hand trembled and she was overtaken by a fit of coughing. She thanked them in a weak voice.

'You shouldn't be doing my work for me. You've your own plates to see to.'

Then one morning Nannie wasn't there, and there was a message brought by a neighbour's boy. 'She's no' well. She says she'll likely be in tomorrow.'

Mr McCracken said nothing as he distributed the pots between Bet and Jess.

'I've enough of my own work to do,' Jess grumbled.

Bet turned on her. 'Oh, be quiet! You're always complaining. Why stay here if you don't like it?'

'I'll maybe not need to work here much longer,' Jess retorted.

The others exchanged glances. Jess was always hinting that her young man would take her away from all this.

Alice paid no attention. What would happen to Nannie? she wondered.

'It's pay day. She'll need her money,' said Bet, a few days later.

Towards the end of the shift, Mr McCracken beckoned Alice over.

'You'll know Nannie – can you take her pay to her? You'll mebbe know where she lives. Anyway, Miss Jenkins in the office will tell you. Away you go now and collect it – and mind you sign for it.'

Alice folded her apron neatly then made her way to the office.

She reached the glass-panelled cubicle where Miss Jenkins sat, adding columns of figures, issuing petty cash slips, entering items in the large leather-bound ledgers. It was set in the centre of the cashiers' office and all round her were the desks where the clerks sat on high stools, adding up columns. In the far corner Alice could see George, concentrating hard on a ledger. She thought of waving to him, but decided against it.

There was someone with Miss Jenkins and to her astonishment, Alice could hear the sound of laughter. Miss Jenkins – laughing? The chief cashier was a middle-aged spinster, invariably dressed in black, her hair in a bun. Her thin fingers whizzed up and down the columns of figures, and she rarely looked up. When you passed through the office, early or late, Miss Jenkins would be there.

Alice sometimes thought she was like one of those German mechanical toys. Turn the key in her back and Miss Jenkins would start nodding, her fingers moving up and down the pages of the ledger, until the mechanism finally wound down late at night and she stopped, and flopped over her desk.

Timidly Alice tapped on the glass, and Miss Jenkins looked round.

'Yes?'

Alice could see that the person with her was a young man with fair curly hair and an open, freckled face.

He said something to Miss Jenkins, and she shook her head at him.

'You're an awful lad, Mr Henry,' she said reprovingly, but with a twinkle in her eye. 'Now get along with you. I've other things to do than listen to your nonsense.'

'Haven't I brightened up your day?' He clapped a hand to his head in comic dismay. 'If not, then it's all been in vain.'

'Mr Henry,' said Miss Jenkins firmly, 'I've told you already – I've better things to do than listen to your blethers. Away you go and wait for your father. He'll not be long. It's near stopping time.'

After he'd gone, she turned to Alice, who was staring after the young man.

'I … I've come for Nannie Macfarlane's wages.' But she was still staring. 'Who was that?'

'Have you not seen him before? That's Mr McCracken's son.'

'Oh, I've heard something about him. He's

not a bit like his father.'

'A clever lad,' said Miss Jenkins approvingly. 'He's at the university now, studying to be a doctor. No wonder his father's proud of him. Mind you, he's a wild lad.' She smiled and shook her head. 'Now then – you want to collect Nannie Macfarlane's wages? Is she not well?'

'She hasn't been in for a few days. She's ill.'

'I hope it's not serious.' Miss Jenkins might look forbidding but she had a warm heart and a soft spot for Nannie. 'There you are. Now you'll sign for it – there.'

Carefully Alice put the envelope into her pocket. She would go to Nicol Street on her way back to Chrissie's house.

As she made her way through the yard, she saw the overseer's son, leaning against a post, joking with one of the men.

'Aye,' said Bet, coming up behind her. 'He's an awful lad.' But she said it with admiration. 'He's quite different from his father – and from his mother, too, by all accounts. A bit wild, but there's no harm in him.'

Alice found Nannie's home easily. In the grey street where the buildings seemed to blot out any sunlight, she shivered despite the warm day. Several children came running up to her.

'I'm looking for Mrs Macfarlane's place,' she told them. 'I've come to see Nannie.'

'Nannie's bad – she's in her bed.' A carroty-haired girl, clearly avid for a piece of gossip, attached herself to Alice.

The woman who opened the door looked elderly, perhaps around seventy, Alice thought. And yet, she must be Nannie's mother.

'Mrs Macfarlane?'

The woman nodded. 'What is it?' She looked suspicious.

'I've come with Nannie's pay.'

The woman's face brightened. 'You'd best come in. She's in her bed.'

It was a hot, stuffy little room. Damp clothes hung over a clothes horse in front of a fire that flickered into life from time to time but mostly sent out clouds of smoke that filled the room. The mantelpiece was crammed with pieces of china, and there were two chairs with the horse-hair hanging out. A table in the centre of the room was covered with an old chenille cloth. In the corner of this overcrowded room was a box bed. The curtains were half drawn but Alice could hear a familiar cough.

'Nannie?'

'Oh, it's you, Alice.' Nannie raised herself on her elbow and smiled. 'My, it's good of you to come.'

Alice could see that it was a great effort for her to speak, and the attempt set off another bout of coughing.

'I brought your pay, and came to see how you are.' Alice found a rickety chair and drew it up beside the bed. 'They're all asking for you,' she went on. 'Even Mr Mc-Cracken.'

Nannie managed a smile, then a cloud seemed to come over her face. 'You shouldn't have come...' she whispered.

'I'm tough,' Alice assured her. 'I'll no catch anything from you.'

'It's not that. I'm not well enough to see to the house and it's...'

Alice put a hand on Nannie's thin forearm. 'You're not to worry about that,' she said cheerfully. 'It doesn't matter,' though she wondered why the mother couldn't clean up a bit. Nannie's mother was sitting by the fire, drinking a cup of tea, and looking morosely into the occasional flames.

'She's never well,' Nannie murmured. 'She needs me to see to things.'

Alice felt a spurt of rage. Nannie's mother was plainly not ill, and, just as clearly, she realised that the woman battened on Nannie.

She glanced around the room. Although it was shabby, the furniture had at one time been of good quality.

'Usually, if we're having a visitor, I can clean up a bit,' Nannie said, before the coughing overtook her again.

'Would you like a drink of water?' Alice offered.

'Thank you. There's a glass on the table.'

As Alice filled the glass, she noticed a piece of embroidery lying unfinished on the table. She picked it up.

'This is pretty. Did you do it?'

Nannie nodded. 'I like sewing. I made the cushions too. Just out of scrap material, mind.'

'They're beautiful.' Alice gazed in admiration at the carefully matched patchwork.

'I'm making a blouse for a friend to wear to a wedding. With embroidery, and trimmed with lace,' Nannie said proudly.

'You are clever,' said Alice, remembering how neatly Nannie worked. 'But here, I'll not tire you. I've put your pay packet on the table.'

But in fact she noticed that the mother

had picked it up, and was eagerly counting the coins.

'Is there anything I can get you?' Alice asked as she rose.

Nannie shook her head. 'It was good of you to come.'

Alice knew what it was like to be poor, but the orphanage had been clean and the orphans encouraged to learn and to work hard. And there had always been enough to eat, though it was dull plain food.

She hadn't seen anything like this squalor.

Was there a way out? Could she find some means of helping poor Nannie?

That evening, as Alice walked with George towards the Park, he turned to her and tucked her hand into the crook of his arm.

'Alice,' he said, 'I know you haven't a mother – but would you like to come and meet mine?'

Alice hesitated. 'Maybe,' she said. 'We'll see.'

How clean he looked, and he smelt of soap – it was one of the first things she had noticed about him. His manners were perfect, too. He always took her arm, lightly by the elbow, as they crossed the road, and lifted his hat when they met.

'Why don't you come to tea next Sunday?'
He gave her arm a little squeeze.

Alice smiled up at him. She was, she told
herself, becoming fond of George.

'My mother will like you,' he told her,
looking approvingly at her fresh complexion,
the wisps of auburn hair on her forehead.
She was different altogether from the other
girls he had met. Alice was open and honest.
Perhaps a little too honest and outspoken,
but that would change.

'I'll call for you about three o'clock on
Sunday,' he promised.

That Sunday Alice sponged and pressed
her best dress and carefully ironed the lace
fichu she had bought with her first wages.
She wished she had a new pair of gloves, but
the old ones, the fingers neatly darned,
would have to do. For a moment, she hesitated – should she wear the necklace that
Mrs Macfee had given her? It was an
amethyst on a slender gold chain.

'You can have that one,' Mrs Macfee had
said carelessly. 'It wouldn't suit my daughter.'

'And,' the woman had told herself, 'it
won't fetch much.'

But Alice decided against the necklace.
She had a feeling that she ought to look

fairly plain. Plain but proud, she thought.

George seemed pleased by her appearance when they met.

'You look nice,' he murmured. 'You'll do me proud.'

The house he took her to was a semi-detached villa, much the same as the other houses in the quiet street – downstairs, two bow-fronted windows, two windows above, and a smaller one just above the front door. The gate swung open at a touch and George led Alice up the front path. There were no flowers here, she noticed, unless you counted a large hydrangea by the gate. Otherwise the front garden was paved over.

She caught a glimpse of a woman standing by the window looking out, and then the figure vanished. Alice smiled to herself. George's mother would not want to appear curious.

'Here we are!' George called as he opened the front door and ushered Alice in.

In the parlour a neat, grey-haired woman sat upright on a high-backed chair, a book in her hand.

'Ah!' She pretended to be surprised. 'So this is Alice.'

She rose and Alice noticed that she was quite tall and rather stately. Her hair was a steel grey and twisted into a bun. She wore a high-necked white blouse, pinned with a cameo brooch, and a grey tweed skirt. The overall impression was just a little intimidating.

'Take your hat off, my dear. George, take Alice's coat.'

George kissed his mother on the cheek. 'And how's my best girl?'

She gave a little moue of pretended protest, which Alice privately thought was rather silly in a woman of her age.

'You won't be saying that much longer, will you?' She looked archly at Alice, who did not respond.

George didn't seem to notice. He hung up Alice's coat and hat, settled his mother in her chair then Alice on the sofa, and finally stretched out in an armchair, holding out his hands to the fire.

'My word, this is cosy!' he said. Alice could almost have said that he purred with pleasure. But to her mind it was not particularly cosy. The room was gloomy, over-stuffed with furniture; small tables held sepia photographs of, she presumed, relatives; the lace curtains shut out the light; and the fire – the flames blinked as if they, too, were discouraged by the atmosphere of gloom.

No, not cosy at all.

Alice had seldom known a more tedious afternoon. George's mother produced photograph albums – 'My late husband', 'George when he was five years old' – and went laboriously through each album, pointing out long-dead aunts and uncles, all of whom seemed to have led exceedingly dull lives. Alice turned the pages politely, waiting for one who had had some thrilling experience – 'This is Uncle Walter, who narrowly escaped being eaten by cannibals', 'This is Aunt Matilda who became the favourite wife of a wealthy sheikh', she said to herself, as George's mother recounted the tedious history of their lives.

The room was stuffy, and Alice almost drowsed off to sleep. She came to with a start, to hear George's mother say, 'But that's enough for now. You must be longing for a cup of tea.'

Alice, balancing a tea cup and a plate, tried not to scatter crumbs of sponge cake on the carpet, and at the same time attempted to listen to Mrs Jamieson's conversation and add the odd murmur of agreement.

At last George said, 'I'll just go and smoke a pipe outdoors.'

'Do that, dear,' said his mother fondly. 'I can't abide the smell of smoke indoors,' she added to Alice. 'My late husband would go outside whatever the weather. Hail or snow,' she said impressively.

'I'll bet he did,' said Alice to herself, smiling politely.

'Now, my dear,' said Mrs Jamieson when the door had closed behind George. 'I hope you and I are going to get to know each other really well. Of course,' she went on, 'you are young, very young. But that doesn't matter. I myself was married at eighteen. Another cup of tea? Yes? Pass your cup.'

Alice would have liked another piece of cake, too, but it was not offered. She wished George would hurry and come back.

'So tell me about your family, my dear,' said George's mother. 'You have no mother of your own, I understand. What does your father do?'

Alice paused. 'I don't know,' she said finally.

The older woman gave a little tinkling laugh. 'Oh, men!' she said. 'They go off to business every morning and we wives and mothers know nothing about what they do.'

'That's not what I meant,' said Alice. 'I meant – I don't know who he was.'

There was a silence.

'I grew up in the orphanage,' Alice added helpfully. 'They didn't tell me anything about my parents.'

'Oh.' Mrs Jamieson's hand fluttered to her throat. 'But ... you would get a good training in the orphanage? You would be well brought up? You went to church and Sunday school, I suppose?'

'Oh, yes,' said Alice. She remembered the dreary march every Sunday to church, the orphans sitting apart from the rest of the children. She remembered, with a spurt of bitterness, a well-dressed girl in a dark blue velvet coat, her hair tied back with a royal blue ribbon, who had pointed to the orphans. 'Poor things, don't they look shabby!' Alice had overheard her say. She flushed at the memory.

'Yes,' she said, 'we were taken to church and to Sunday school.'

'You would be well trained?' her hostess went on. 'In housework, cookery and schooling?'

'Oh, yes, I can read and write and mind my manners. We were well trained, we charity girls,' Alice agreed with an edge to her voice.

'I'm sure you were...' Mrs Jamieson was at

a loss. 'And when you left, you went into service?'

Alice nodded. 'Yes, I was in service. To Miss Elsie Macintosh ... till she died.'

Mrs Jamieson brightened. 'I knew of her. A fine old lady, and a very respectable family. You would have good training there.'

Alice said nothing. Certainly she had been trained to scrub floors and carry trays and be at the beck and call of her employer.

'So the house was sold after the old lady died?' Mrs Jamieson could not resist asking.

'I suppose so.'

'Were there relatives?'

'A niece.'

'Ah, and I suppose she would inherit?' It was a question, rather than a statement, and Alice smiled inwardly. She knew that Mrs Jamieson was trying to pump her for information which she could then pass on: 'I heard, my dear, from a very reliable source...'

'I don't really know,' said Alice. 'I expect she did.'

'I wonder...' George's mother did not quite know how to put it. 'I wonder that she did not leave something to you?' Did this girl have money? Probably not. Otherwise why was she working in the pottery?

Alice was not going to enter into any discussion with this woman to satisfy her curiosity, so she smiled politely and said nothing.

'So, you are working in the pottery, George tells me?' Mrs Jamieson gave up her enquiries and tried another tack. 'That must be tedious work. Among girls who are...' She was about to say 'not our class', when it occurred to her that she did not know what class Alice belonged to.

'I have some good friends,' Alice said staunchly. She decided suddenly that she had had enough of this woman and her impudent questions. 'And, of course, I expect to be promoted.'

'Indeed? To another part of the pottery?'

'I fully expect,' said Alice, furtively crossing her fingers, 'to be a full decorator before very long.'

'That will be well paid, no doubt,' said the older woman.

'I expect so,' said Alice carelessly. 'But earning a great deal of money is not my main aim in life. I intend to succeed as an artist. And, as you must know,' she added wickedly, 'artists never make any money. They also live a rather–' she paused '–a rather unconventional life.'

Alice was quite proud of her vocabulary.

She had always enjoyed reading and regularly brought books home from the local library. Now her efforts had been rewarded, she thought, watching the effect of the word 'unconventional' on her hostess.

'Indeed,' said George's mother.

The girl was a little unusual – certainly not as humble or as grateful as she might have hoped. She thought wistfully of the nicely brought-up girls, the daughters of friends, who were content to sit at home and embroider, and take an interest in good causes. But still, Alice was young, and could be moulded to be a fit wife for George. If she was George's choice.

'More tea, my dear?' Mrs Jamieson refilled Alice's cup and placed it on the little table by Alice's chair. Alice turned to look longingly at the plate of sponge cake ... and nudged her cup with her elbow.

'Oh!' She sprang up, dismayed, watching the tea spread over the carpet, and scrubbing furiously at the stain on the cretonne cover of the chair. 'I'm so sorry!' She blushed, and her confidence ebbed away fast.

'It's quite all right, my dear.' Her hostess rose. 'Don't you trouble about it. I'll just get a cloth and mop up. George!' she called to her son.

'What is it?' George appeared at the door. 'A cloth, dear, if you will.'

The mopping-up took some time and all the while Alice stood by, murmuring apologies.

And then it was time to go. Alice shook hands with George's mother, and took a deep breath as they walked down the path. She felt sure Mrs Jamieson was watching from the window.

'It doesn't matter,' George told her as he escorted her home.

'Of course it doesn't,' said Alice crossly. 'It was only a cup of tea spilt, for goodness sake.' She stopped and looked up at him. 'George, why didn't you tell your mother I came from the orphanage?'

'Because it doesn't matter a scrap.' He took her face between his hands. 'Because you are my dear Alice, no matter where you came from.'

Alice was reassured. Oh, perhaps his mother was a snob, but she had met people like Mrs Jamieson before now. She could hold her own with that type. And George – well, he was handsome, and kind. Look how patient he was with his mother. He didn't seem to notice that she was difficult and demanding. For a charity girl, he would be a fine husband. I would be the luckiest girl in the whole world, Alice told herself.

Chrissie was sitting at the kitchen table, a newspaper spread out before her, when Alice got home.

'Well, lass, did you have a good time?'

'Yes,' said Alice non-committally. She glanced at the newspaper. 'I thought you couldn't read?'

'I can't. I've been waiting for you to come back. You'll maybe read the advertisements to me.'

'What do you want to know?'

'It's the situations vacant, lass,' said Chrissie. 'Now that I've got you lending a hand with the mending and that, I could take on more work. See if you can find anyone that's wanting washing done, or anyone looking for a cleaner. Or maybe there's a young man seeking respectable lodgings. You could write me a reference.'

Alice picked up the Fife Free Press and skimmed the advertisements.

'You could get a job in the linen mill,' she pointed out.

Chrissie shook her head. 'I'm too old now. No, cleaning's what I'm best at, and washing.'

'Well...' Alice hesitated. Then her eye was

caught by an advertisement: *Girl to learn sewing wanted. Three shillings a week. Apply Miss Todd...*

She'd heard some of the girls talk about Miss Todd. A top-class dressmaker, she made gowns and mantles for some of the wealthy ladies in the town.

She read the advertisement again.

'Have you found anything?' Chrissie wanted to know.

'I don't know,' Alice said slowly. 'I just might have.'

Chapter Five

A Big Decision

'I've got a plan for Nannie,' said Alice mysteriously, as she and Bet made their way along Oswald Street towards the pottery. It was a fine spring morning. Even here, in the fine late March days, dusty shrubs had begun to look fresh and new. 'It's a secret, as yet,' she went on.

Something was wrong with Bet, she thought, astonished. Normally Bet loved secrets, and would sit close to Alice, whispering and giggling. But today–

'You haven't heard a thing I've been saying. What's the matter? Is there something wrong at home?'

And yet how could there be anything wrong in that noisy household, where there was a vast crowd of brothers and sisters and cousins to laugh and argue happily together? Alice envied them; it must be wonderful, she thought wistfully, to have brothers and sisters.

'Nothing's wrong,' said Bet dreamily.

Alice looked at her again. 'Oh, I see. It's a lad, isn't it?'

She tried to remember what Bet had said about the fisher lads she knew, about the raucous jokes, and the lively nights dancing when the boats came in to harbour. About rising early to see the boats setting off for the North Sea. About the superstitions – Alice pretended to scoff, but she knew Bet took them seriously.

'His name's Jackie. We've got an understanding,' Bet confided shyly.

For a moment Alice felt something like sadness, and realised swiftly that it was almost jealousy, because love could make her friend – down-to-earth, no-nonsense Bet – behave like this.

'You haven't met him,' said Bet. 'But there's a dance in Dysart on Saturday. You'll see him then, if you come. And you could bring your lad.' She sounded a little doubtful. They'd all seen George waiting for Alice at the end of the day, and there was a fair amount of good-natured teasing in the shed. But George was office staff, a bit too grand maybe for a dance in the hall at Dysart.

'There's to be a band, and lemonade and cakes...'

'I'll see,' said Alice quickly. But she was excited at the thought. She had never been to a dance. Miss Macintosh had disapproved of dancing, though at the orphanage some of the girls had practised waltzing, whirling round the hall when the matron wasn't looking.

'What's he like, your Jackie?'

'He's very handsome. And he's going to get his own boat, and then we'll be married. He's saving up for a ring.'

Alice gave her friend's arm a squeeze. 'Good for you,' she said. 'Come on now, we'll be late. And see you don't go daydreaming about your Jackie, or you'll be breaking even more plates than usual.'

Everyone, even Chrissie, seemed to accept that Alice and George were courting, even though they had been out together only a few times – to a concert, or for an evening stroll in Beveridge Park.

'Take your time. You're young yet,' Chrissie warned. She had met George briefly. 'He's a handsome lad, I'll give you that,' she commented.

Alice pretended not to hear her. She was aware of how handsome George was – he was like one of the tall, dark heroes in the novelettes that Bet liked to read – and of how smartly dressed he was. He stood out, Alice thought, from the other young men in the wages office.

When Alice next saw George, at home time that evening, she said casually, 'There's a dance on Saturday. And Bet's asked us to go. It's along at Dysart. There's going to be a band – accordions. They'll have reels – the eightsome, of course, and the Lancers.'

'I don't know.' George hesitated. 'I've heard about these dances – they can get a bit rowdy.'

'The lads just like a bit of fun – and so would you if you had such a tough life,' said Alice firmly.

'If you want to go to a dance,' said George,

103

'there's a social evening at our church hall in a fortnight's time.'

Alice was exasperated. 'That's not the same thing at all.' Even though she had never been to a dance, she knew this one would be quite different from a decorous church social.

'Going to a fishermen's dance,' George insisted, 'it's not the thing for a young lady.'

'Oh, for goodness sake, George!' Alice stopped in the middle of the street and glared at him. 'That's stupid... Don't be such a snob.'

She expected him to apologise, perhaps to reason with her. Or even to smile and turn her comments away. Instead, he became very quiet, and said, 'Well, Alice, if that's how you see me there's no more to be said.'

And he turned and walked away.

Alice, horrified at what she had said, was about to run after him. But she was too shocked. She wanted to say she was sorry, but something – pride maybe – held her back. She simply stood in the middle of the dusty road, willing him to turn round. Then she'd say she hadn't meant it, and everything would be all right again. But he didn't turn round.

In the days that followed, Alice half expected

George to call at Chrissie's, to say it was all a misunderstanding, and that of course he would come to the dance with her. But she knew he wouldn't. He had his pride, too.

Alice went to the dance on her own. However, Bet and Jackie seemed to know everyone and she had no shortage of partners.

'Would you like to do the eightsome?' Alice looked up at the tall young man with the top of curly hair. He leaned against a pillar and grinned at her. 'Mind you, it can get a bit hearty.'

'I don't know how to do this one,' Alice confessed.

'Come on.' He held out a hand. 'It's not that difficult. I'll show you.'

Whirling round, Alice hardly had time to think beyond being aware that she was enjoying herself. At the end, flushed and exhilarated, she gasped for breath.

'I'll get you a bottle of lemonade,' said her partner.

Alice sipped gratefully at the drink, but when she turned to thank him, he had gone.

'My, but this is a great night,' said Bet, joining her. Her hair had come unpinned and her eyes sparkled.

Alice envied Bet, clutching Jackie's arm and giggling. He was tall, with a shock of black hair, a strong, jutting jaw and thick black eyebrows.

'He looks a bit like a pirate,' Alice thought, smiling inwardly. 'All he needs is an eye patch.'

But there was nothing piratical about Jackie. He was slow-spoken; in fact, he didn't say very much, except, 'Aye', and, 'Fine that', and Alice wondered how he had ever plucked up the courage to propose to Bet. But there was no doubt about his feelings for her – it was plain on his face as he looked down at her, beaming proudly.

For the next few days, Alice felt miserable. She knew she had been unkind to George. 'But he was being snobbish,' she told herself. 'And he doesn't own me.'

All the same, he *had* been kind, and if he was a bit too serious, well, who could blame him with a mother like that?

'I could change that,' she thought. 'I could make him laugh.'

'You won't get the chance now,' said her other self.

When they passed each other on the way into work, or going home, George would nod politely, then look the other way.

'Oh, well,' thought Alice, 'that's that. It's over. I was too hasty.'

Now, however, she had other things to think about. She had carefully read and re-read the advertisement in Chrissie's newspaper. And a few days later, she decided.

It was late in the day, after work, when Alice made her way to the address given in the newspaper.

'There's no harm in trying,' she told herself firmly, as she pressed the shining brass bell push.

For a few minutes there was silence, and then she could hear rapid footsteps, and the door was opened by a tiny grey-haired woman, a tape measure round her neck, and a pad stuck with pins on her wrist. She looked at Alice enquiringly.

'Well? What can I do for you?'

'I've come about the advertisement in the paper. You want someone to sew.'

'Ah, yes. I am Miss Todd. You'd better come in.' The little woman held the door open. 'Follow me,' she said briskly, leading the way into the back premises.

The latest Singer sewing machine stood on a table by the window. Another table held swathes of fabric, and shelves around the room were piled with feathers, flowers and bows of satin and lace. Around the room, too, hung several dresses which were almost finished, and Alice caught her breath as she admired the delicate silks and soft velvets.

The dressmaker herself was dressed in a rather shabby black costume, and wore pince-nez on the end of her nose.

'Now,' she said in the same no-nonsense tone, 'sit down–' she pointed to a bentwood chair. 'I'll just finish cutting out this sleeve. I am never idle,' she went on. 'All day – and well into the evening – I work. People say to me, "Why do you drive yourself so hard?" It is my nature,' she said solemnly. 'I toil with eager hands.'

Alice did not quite know what to say, so she continued to look around with interest.

Immediately her eye was caught by a dress that hung on a dressmaker's dummy in the centre of the room.

It was the most beautiful dress Alice had ever seen, a slender dress of cream silk, trimmed with inserts of lace. It had leg-of-mutton sleeves ending in a pleated cuff, and the low neck was softened by a fichu of georgette in a delicate apricot shade.

'That's lovely,' said Alice. She could hardly take her eyes off the dress.

The dressmaker laid down her scissors. 'It

took a great deal of work,' said Miss Todd proudly. 'See–' She showed Alice the stitching on the bodice, and the inserts of lace.

'Of course, it is for a very special customer. Miss Harrower – such a delightful young woman. She's sailing next week on a wonderful new liner. Such a voyage! And there will be dancing every night. My Miss Harrower will be the belle of the ball, no doubt about that.' She beamed with pride, and Alice, too, imagined the elegant young woman, the vast ballroom ablaze with electric light, the orchestra playing the latest waltzes, and Miss Harrower's partners, queuing to fill in her dance card. And Miss Harrower herself – fair-haired, possibly, with a fringe of curls on her forehead, her blue eyes sparkling, flirting with her admirers.

The dressmaker tweaked the skirt of the dress. 'Yes, I think this is one of the finest dresses I've made.'

She became brisk and picked up a piece of cloth. 'Now, I shall have to see what you can do. I'd like you to finish this row of hemstitching.'

Alice looked blankly at her. 'But...'

'Come along,' said Miss Todd. 'Don't be bashful. You can't expect me to employ you without seeing how well you can sew, can you?'

'But–' Alice stammered '–I'm not applying for the job.'

'Then why,' said the dressmaker, puzzled, 'are you here?'

'It's for a friend of mine,' Alice explained, and she told Miss Todd about Nannie.

'She sews most beautifully. Patchwork, cushions, a blouse for a friend. And it would be so much better for her health than working in the pottery. All the dust isn't good for her chest. And some of the girls, they're a bit hard on her, because sometimes she can't keep up with the rest.' She wondered if she had said too much. She didn't want Miss Todd to think that Nannie was someone who couldn't manage a regular job.

The dressmaker pursed her lips. 'I see.'

For a moment, Alice thought she was going to say, 'She wouldn't be at all suitable. I couldn't possibly take her on.'

Instead Miss Todd said thoughtfully, 'I have lots of girls who want to come and work for me. But I must have someone who will learn quickly. I can't just take on anyone.' For a moment she looked quite fierce.

'Yes,' said Alice humbly. 'Yes, I know.'

'Wait a minute.' She looked closely at Alice. 'So you have come to interview me, is that it? You want to see if I'd be a suitable employer for your friend, eh?' For a moment she looked as if she might be cross, then her eyes twinkled. 'Tell her to come and see me after work tomorrow. I do need someone to train up. We'll find out if she would suit.'

'Oh, thank you!' Alice felt a great surge of relief.

'Remember,' said Miss Todd, 'she must be good, and hardworking, and come up to my standards, which are very, very high.'

'I know,' said Alice. 'I'm sure she'll work hard, and she sews beautifully.'

'Very well. Off you go.' The interview was at an end, and the little dressmaker turned back to her work table.

Alice skipped down the stairs. Oh, this was such an opportunity for Nannie. She could hardly wait to tell her friend.

'I have some news for you,' Alice whispered to Nannie at the dinner break. 'Come outside – I don't want the others to hear.'

Nannie closed her piece tin, and followed Alice outside.

'What is it? Has something nice happened to you?'

111

'Not to me,' said Alice dramatically. 'It's about you.'

Nannie listened open-mouthed as Alice explained.

'But would I be good enough? It sounds just the sort of job I'd like, working with those lovely materials. But...'

'No buts,' Alice said firmly. 'You go and see Miss Todd.' She had a sudden thought. 'You *can* do hem-stitching, can't you?'

Nannie smiled. 'Of course. It sounds too good to be true. I don't know how to thank you.'

'Wait till you've got the job – *then* you can thank me. Come on, there's the bell.'

Nannie's pale face was flushed with excitement. 'Oh, I can't wait...'

Jess watched the two girls as they made their way back into the shed.

'And what are you two up to?' she said, coming up behind Alice.

'Nothing that's any of your business,' said Alice sharply.

'I wonder,' said Jess with a half-smile. 'I wonder.' She turned aside, and went into the shed.

It was a whole week later before Alice found George waiting for her at the works gate.

She was about to nod politely and sidestep him, as usual, but he stood firmly in her way.

'Will you come for a walk this evening?'

Bet gave her a nudge and a broad grin, and went on ahead.

'Yes, if you like.'

'I thought we'd go to the beach.'

'Yes, of course.' They had still not got back to their former easy friendship. And yet, she thought, it was stupid to behave like this. Everyone had tiffs. Look at Bet and Jackie. They were always falling out, and for a day or two Bet would go around sighing and looking miserable. Then they would make up, and Alice could always tell when they had for Bet would sing and hum as she spun the pots around on her stand.

So, a mild tiff meant nothing. It would be good to be real friends again. And George *was* a friend, steady and kind and thoughtful.

'All right. I'm sorry about what I said,' she added. 'I didn't mean it.'

George smiled and felt reassured. 'Don't give it another thought.'

Alice took particular trouble with her appearance that evening. Bet, always generous, had passed on a black straw boater to her; Alice had been going to save it for a special occasion, but she tried it on, and it was becoming.

'You look nice,' said George, when he arrived. That was another thing about him. He always noticed how you looked, or if you were cold or chilled, or under the weather.

'Thank you.' Alice put her arm through his. She could do this now; after many months, they were an established couple. One day, perhaps – but Alice pushed the thought away. She didn't want to make plans ahead.

Oh, how thankful she was that the tiff was behind them. She would be more careful in future, and guard her tongue.

They took the road down to the sea front, and George turned to look admiringly at Alice as a slight breeze ruffled her hair. The tide was going out, and small waves lapped at the wet ripples on the sand.

Alice was silent, and George patted the hand that was tucked into the crook of his arm. Immediately, Alice withdrew her hand and, clutching the new straw hat, tripped along the sand. She bent to pick up a stone.

'Let's see if I can make this skip!' she said.

She flung the stone and it danced in a series of little leaps across the surface of the water.

'Oh!' she cried out with almost childish delight. 'I wonder if I can do that again?'

'Alice!' George called after her, but she was running over the sands, turning to call out to him, 'Come on, let's race!'

Reluctantly George followed her, until he caught her up. Breathless, she pulled off the new straw hat and looked up at him, her eyes shining.

He held her in his arms, until she twisted out of his grasp.

'Alice, please,' he said. 'Let's just walk. I want to talk to you.'

Swinging her hat in one hand, she allowed George to hold her other hand firmly, and they strolled back the way they had come.

'Listen, Alice.' George stopped suddenly and turned to face her. 'We've not known each other long but we get on well together. I know you're young...'

'I'm nearly eighteen,' Alice broke in. 'And when I'm older, I'll be able to vote. Mrs Pankhurst has promised that one day, every woman will have the right to vote.'

For a moment George hesitated. Then he plunged on.

'Never mind votes for women. That's not important...'

'Not–? But it's *very* important...' she

protested, but then she broke off when she saw his face. He really was serious and she would not hurt him by teasing him any more.

'My mother likes you – and you like her...'

'Ye-es,' said Alice a little guardedly.

'I know she's a bit possessive of me, but that needn't matter to us, as long as we're sure of each other, I mean.'

He stumbled over the words, and Alice remembered how kind, how patient he was with his mother. How he thought all the time about her comfort, and never objected to her demands.

'I hope she realises what a good son he is,' she thought.

'Yes?' she prompted gently.

'What I'm trying to say, Alice, is that I love you. Would you marry me? Not immediately, mind,' he added hastily. 'I'd have to save a bit first, make a real home for you. But would you, Alice?'

'Don't keep me waiting too long for your answer,' George had said, and Alice tossed and turned all night, trying to decide.

In the morning she woke heavy-eyed. Chrissie couldn't help noticing.

'That lad of yours has been keeping you

116

up too late,' she said with a wink. Alice, tired of Chrissie's nods and hints, said nothing.

At work she found it hard to concentrate, and she was preoccupied when she joined Bet at break time. Bet was her usual cheerful self.

'Some of the fisher lads at the dance have been asking about you,' she told her. 'They want to know if you're courting. Are you?'

'That's my business,' Alice snapped.

'All right, Miss High and Mighty,' said Bet, offended, and she rose with dignity and took her tin and her bread and cheese over to join Nell, who was talking non-stop about her plans for a visit to an aunt.

'Oh, how could I?' Alice reproached herself. Bet was such a good friend. But when she looked across at Bet, the other girl ignored her and seemed to be listening intently to Nell's chatter.

Alice went back to work feeling low in spirit. If this was what romance meant, she didn't want any part of it!

And now she had no plans for Sunday, while all the other girls seemed to be busy with family or friends. Alice had told George very firmly that she couldn't meet him at the weekend.

'It's best we don't see each other for a day

or two, George. It'll give me time to think things over.'

He'd looked rather downcast. 'What am I going to do without you?' he'd said, making her feel guilty.

'You could take your mother out somewhere,' she'd suggested.

'That's not the same and you know it. But, well, maybe I will.'

And she thought again how kind and thoughtful he was. There was none of the coarseness of some of the fisher lads, or the young men who worked in a pottery. The perfect gentleman, that was George.

She decided that she wouldn't waste the day. If it was fine, she would take her sketch pad out somewhere, into one of the villages maybe, or into the country.

She imagined George's horror if she told him of her plans, and how he would insist on coming with her.

As she waited for the bus, clutching her sketchbook, Alice thought again of the tiff with Bet. She hadn't meant to snub her friend, but if only Bet and the other girls were not so concerned with young men – who was courting, who had broken up, whose nose had been put out of joint. Alice found it tiresome, and yet, she didn't want to seem standoffish. She knew they'd thought her a bit aloof to begin with.

'Who does she think she is? She's just a charity girl,' she recalled Nell saying in a voice that had been meant to be overheard.

And yet, she was just the same as them, except she had no parents, no-one in the world. There was only George...

She pushed the thought away. There was time enough to make up her mind. Today was for enjoying the sunshine and looking at the wild flowers growing along the roadside, and appreciating the peace and quiet after the noise and clamour of the works.

Oh, this was perfect, she thought, as she felt the light breeze ruffle her hair. She wandered along the village's main street, looking at the cottages, one with a scarlet geranium in the window, another with a tortoiseshell cat sunning itself in a door-way.

A woman, shaking a mat outside her door, paused and called out, 'It's a grand day.'

'It certainly is,' Alice agreed. 'Is this the way to the beach?'

'Keep straight on,' the woman told her, then added, 'Would you look at they bairns. I've just washed that bit!'

Alice turned to see a group of children

marking out the squares for a game of peevers.

Later that day, back at her lodgings, Alice looked at the sketches she had done – the pink campion, the scarlet poppies, the sweep of the sand dunes. She could still feel the salt air on her cheeks and, remembering the day, she began to paint.

However, she soon flung down her brush in a fit of exasperation.

'I'll never be good enough,' she told herself. 'If only I could afford good paints and a set of brushes – and an easel.' And then she caught herself up. 'Don't be stupid,' she thought. 'If you're any good at all, you'll make a success of it, whatever your tools. It isn't sable brushes that make an artist. Though it helps...'

She looked with distaste at the old paint box she had found in a second-hand shop, and remembered gratefully the first paint box she had had. Who could that anonymous gift have been from? Could it have been Miss Lennox? She was the only person Alice had ever known who was interested in art.

She looked at her painting again with a critical eye.

'It's not bad,' she thought, 'but not good enough. I need someone to teach me. I suppose I could save up for lessons. I'm certainly not going to get any better by myself,' she declared. 'This is a daub – that's all.'

And then she remembered George. Maybe if she and George were married, she could paint full-time, and maybe there would be enough money for paints.

Instantly she was horrified at herself. 'You've come mercenary, Alice! Fancy considering a proposal in that way.'

But no, she decided, she wouldn't be marrying George for his money. He wasn't rich by any means – not yet. Certainly he had a comfortable home and a modest salary as a clerk, but George had ambition, she knew. He'd talked about getting another job, studying for exams. He would make his way in life.

They had never spoken much about her painting, she remembered. And there weren't any paintings in his slightly depressing home, just large sepia photographs of relations.

'If it was my house,' she thought, 'I'd get rid of all that gloomy furniture and those heavy velvet curtains. I'd have simple pieces and bright fabrics.' Fabrics like the William Morris patterns she'd seen in a shop.

121

'George and I – we'd make a good partnership,' she thought. How kind he was, how thoughtful. That counted for a great deal.

'Don't keep me waiting,' he had said. Well, she had made up her mind.

Next evening, George called for her. 'A walk in the park maybe?' he said. 'It's a fine evening.'

As usual he tucked her hand into the crook of his arm, and smiled down at her. 'You're looking very pretty tonight,' he said. 'But then, you always do.'

They walked along companionably, laughing at a small boy bowling a hoop along the street, and his mother shouting from a window that it was time to come indoors. A pink rose overhanging a wall made Alice skirt round it but then she stopped to try to catch its perfume.

'Not much scent,' she said. 'Not like the dark red roses. But it's pretty all the same.'

'I would like to buy you roses,' said George all of a sudden. 'Lots of them.'

Alice suddenly felt uneasy, and turned the conversation.

'At the weekend I took a bus to the seaside and made some sketches in the dunes. Gemmell Hutchinson's wonderful painting of the seashore that's what I was trying to capture. You can almost smell the sea, and feel the sharpness of the stalks of grass…'

'I don't care much for art,' said George dismissively. 'And you know, Alice, that you shouldn't go off on your own…'

'I was perfectly safe,' she said, a little crossly, and then felt ashamed of herself. He was only trying to protect her, after all.

'Well, it's a nice hobby for a young lady, at least,' said George. 'I've no objection to your sketching. Lots of ladies do.'

'But – but I don't want to be a genteel lady doing nice little sketches,' Alice flared up. 'I want to be a real artist.'

'Oh, my dear Alice,' said George. 'That takes time and training. Wouldn't it be better to enjoy sketching as a hobby? After all, once we're married, you won't have time for drawing and painting, what with running a home, looking after me…'

Alice stood stock still and stared at him.

'And you know you've promised to give me your answer soon. Don't keep me waiting too long, will you?'

Alice drew a deep breath. Suddenly she could see the future mapped out very clearly – and it wasn't a future she wanted for herself. George was kind and caring, and he would make a good husband, but for someone else. 'We belong in different worlds,' she thought.

'George,' she said carefully, 'I *have* thought it over. I'm very honoured by your proposal, and I am truly touched that you should want me for your wife – but I can't marry you. I don't love you – at least, not enough. So I'm sorry, George, but the answer is no.'

Chapter Six

Bad News For Bet

'You'll come to the harbour when the boats sail,' said Bet. 'You'll see Jackie's boat – the *Spindrift*. Well,' she added honestly, 'it's not actually his. He's one of the fishermen. But one day he'll have a boat of his own, that's for sure.'

The quay was crowded with families. Someone was playing an accordion, and young children, clutching their mothers' hands, gazed with wonder at the boats.

Several young boys raced in and out of the crowd, sometimes tripping over the ropes, while the fishermen roared at them, 'Get out of the way, ye limmers!' The crews hurried back and forth, shouting last-minute instructions, shoving curious bystanders out of the way. There were a number of older women, huddled into shawls, chatting together, and remembering past stories of the boats and the crews.

Alice shivered in the cold air and tucked her hands into her sleeves.

'Will they be away long?' she asked Bet.

'A week or so.' Bet's eyes were fixed on Jackie's boat. 'They go up the coast. There's more cod there.'

A tall, swarthy man with a thick black beard jumped on to the quay and began shouting orders to the crew.

'That's Angus – he's the skipper,' said Bet in an undertone. 'They're all feared of him.'

Now a thin, rather weedy youth began loading fish boxes.

'That's the lad – Hamish,' said Jackie, appearing beside the two girls. 'It's his first trip.'

Before he could say anything else, a stout woman still wearing a pinafore, shawl wrapped round her head, pushed her way on to the quay. 'Where is he? Where's Hamish?'

Suddenly she spotted her son.

'You went away without your jersey,' she scolded him. 'I've not spent all winter knitting this for you to leave it behind. See the pattern – it's a proper gansey.'

The skipper turned round in exasperation. 'We're about to sail, missus. You shouldn't be on the boat.'

She was not at all put out. 'He'll maybe be glad of the jersey,' she said sternly.

'Oh, aye,' said the skipper dryly. 'Ah, well, it's kindly meant. Now, missus,' he said, 'we're near casting off, so move back out of the road.'

She sniffed but did as she was told, joining the crowd that was watching from a distance, craning for a last glimpse of the boats.

'We'll not be that long away.' Jackie was about to give Bet a peck on the cheek, but she flung her arms around him.

'Look after yourself and come back soon,' she said.

'I've no' forgotten about the ring,' he said. 'When I come back.'

Alice turned away, not wanting to intrude, but she felt a little pang of envy. One day, maybe, she would have a lad of her own.

'I'd best be getting on board.' Jackie glanced over Bet's shoulder. 'The skipper gets wild if we're late sailing.'

One old man in the crowd wasn't looking at the boats. His eyes were fixed on the sky. 'See those clouds? There's a storm on the way.'

No one paid any attention to him. They were all craning for a last look at the men who were setting off. The accordionist began playing softly – Alice recognised the mournful tune of 'Caller Herrin' – and someone told him to 'Play something cheerier, man.'

As the *Spindrift* sailed out of the harbour, Jackie gave a wave from the deck. Bet called out, 'Hurry back,' and waved her scarf until the boat was far out of sight, then turned away with a little sigh.

'Come on,' said Alice. 'Let's treat ourselves to tea and buns.'

Bet put away her handkerchief. 'And he'll soon be back. I'll need to get used to seeing him off. I'm going to start knitting a gansey for him. That'll keep me busy while he's away.'

'A gansey?'

'A fisherman's sweater. They each have their own pattern – so that…' She bit her lip and didn't continue. She didn't want to dwell on the fact that a fisherman lost at sea could be identified by the pattern of his gansey.

Determinedly she smiled. 'I'm hungry. Did you say buns with jam?'

A week later, there was talk of storms up north, but Bet seemed unconcerned.

'Jackie'll be all right,' she said. 'We'll go and see the boats come in.'

Her eyes sparkled. These days she was always preoccupied. More than once, Alice, watching from the other end of the shed, had seen the overseer speak to her.

She knew why Bet had that far-away look, and she tried her hardest to be pleased for her friend and listen attentively when she talked about the wedding plans.

'We'll have a show of presents,' Bet told her. 'My auntie's giving us a canteen of cutlery, and my granny's been sewing us a patchwork quilt.'

'And I'll give you china – that's the bridesmaid's present.' Alice smiled. 'Will you miss working here?' she asked.

Bet made a face. 'Not me.'

'But being a fisherman's wife, you'll have to mend nets and bait hooks.' Alice shuddered. 'I wouldn't like that.'

Again Bet's face took on that contented expression. 'But I'll be Jackie's wife,' she said, 'and that'll make up for anything.'

This time Alice felt ever so slightly jealous. But she pushed the feeling away. She had never felt anything remotely like this for George.

George – Alice smiled to herself, thinking how anxious she'd been that she had broken his heart. But George hadn't missed her for long. Just last Sunday she had met him walking sedately along the High Street with a young woman she recognised from the church. The young woman had clung to his arm and looked up into his face with clear adoration. George had looked greatly pleased with himself. As they passed, he had lifted his head and said, 'Good afternoon.'

'Who was that?' Alice had heard the girl ask.

'Just someone from the works,' George had replied. And Alice had smiled to herself. He hadn't taken long to get over his grand passion, she'd thought, and this girl was obviously more suitable.

But now – well, it would be pleasant to be as starry-eyed as Bet, to be planning a wedding, though Alice didn't really want all the frills. 'I'm not used to that kind of thing,' she thought.

The other girls teased Bet about her romance. Most were glad for her – Bet was well-liked. Only Jess, secure in the devotion of her own young man, was indifferent.

'You'd think she was the only one had got a lad,' she sniffed, and then went on to grumble about work.

Alice, happily engrossed in her new job working with transfers, paid little attention. It was a busy time, especially now that Nannie, quiet and hard-working, had left.

Alice smiled as she thought of the girl as she'd seen her last week, in the dressmaker's workroom. They were like two little mice, Miss Todd and her new assistant. Nannie sat stitching steadily, hardly raising her eyes from her work, while Miss Todd kept up a running commentary on what she was doing. 'Now this collar, it needs to be set just so.' 'Another dart just here on the bodice.'

'She's that kind,' said Nannie later in a burst of confidence. 'She says I'm too thin, and I've to be fed up. So I get milk and home-made scones at my break.' She beamed happily. 'And I'm to get to help with a wedding dress.'

It was a bleak afternoon, when Bet and Alice stood together on the quayside.

'Good thing it's the half-day,' said Bet, tucking her arm through Alice's. 'I'd not like to miss Jackie coming home.' Her eyes shone and she hopped from one foot to the other with excitement.

'They'll have done well, this trip,' said an old man waiting in the crowd. 'There's plenty of cod up the coast.'

'When he gets back,' Bet confided to Alice, 'Jackie's going to buy me a ring. Maybe a diamond.' She held out her left hand, imagining the ring on her finger. 'Then we'll be properly engaged.' She smiled contentedly.

As they stood waiting, the *Spindrift* appeared out of the mist. 'There she is!' Bet squealed.

The skipper of the *Spindrift* jumped ashore as soon as the boat tied up at the quay.

'Where's Jackie's lass?' His eyes scanned the quayside, looking for Bet.

She hurried forward. 'What's the matter, Angus? Has something happened?'

'Now you're not to worry,' he said, but his face was serious. 'He's had a wee bit of an accident, your Jackie. We'll need to get a doctor to him – fast.'

'Let me...' Bet would have rushed on to the boat, but he put out a restraining arm.

'No, lass, you'll only hold things up. Wait till he's safe ashore.'

The crowd parted and someone went

hurrying up into the village to bring the doctor back.

Bet clutched at her friend's arm. 'What if he's hurt bad? What if he's...'

'Now,' Alice put an arm round Bet. 'Don't go fretting. Wait till the doctor sees him.'

The doctor came hurrying through the crowd and it seemed an age till he climbed ashore again.

Bet rushed forward. 'What's happened? Why can't I see him?'

'Are you his lass?' The doctor looked at her kindly, his usually stern expression softening. 'You'll see him in a minute. He's asking for you.'

'Then he's alive...'

'Aye.' The doctor paused. 'But he's been badly knocked about. He's a brave lad. Seems he jumped into the sea to rescue the young one when he was knocked overboard by a wave.'

A crowd had gathered, listening as the doctor went on. 'Your Jackie got caught in the lines trying to get back...'

'And the young lad?' someone asked.

'He's all right. He was lucky.'

He turned to the boat and gave a quiet command to the crew. 'You can bring him ashore now. Steady though – don't jolt him if you can help it.'

They laid the stretcher on the quayside, and Bet knelt down beside it.

'Jackie...' she said brokenly.

Jackie managed a faint smile. 'Eh, lass,' he said.

Several people surged forward to help Bet to her feet, and she followed the stretcher as Jackie was borne away.

Alice, about to go with her, felt a hand on her arm.

'He's tough is Jackie – he'll not be beaten.' It was the tall, curly-haired young man Alice had met at the dance in Dysart, the one who had got her some lemonade and then disappeared. 'I'll come with you and see you both safe home,' he added. 'You're Bet's friend?'

Alice could only nod. He put a hand under her elbow.

'Come on then. Move back there,' he ordered the crowd of women who stood watching, their shawls tightly wrapped around them.

Alice hurried along, glad of his firm grip on her arm.

'Will he be all right?' she asked tremulously. 'It would be terrible for Bet if anything happened.' Her voice shook.

'Aye, well.' The tall young man glanced

down at her. 'We're tough, us fisher folk. And Jackie's as strong as a horse. But–' he paused '–he's hurt bad,' he conceded. 'We'll need to wait and see.'

Jackie's convalescence was a long, slow business. His right leg, badly broken, was slow to heal and would leave him with a permanent limp. There could be no question of him going back to sea.

'It's the only thing he knows,' Bet confided sadly one day. She was quiet now. In the past her shrieks of laughter would echo round the shed and earn disapproving looks from the overseer, but now, when the girls gathered for their break, she would sit quietly nursing a mug of cocoa, and taking little part in the conversation around her.

Alice badly wanted to do something to help, but it seemed there was very little she could do or say.

Jess and her young man were courting, and Jess could talk of nothing but the approaching wedding, the show of presents, the bridesmaids she'd chosen.

'My aunt's giving us her best china,' she said importantly one day. 'She says it's no use for her so we might as well have it. It's painted with violets, and it's got gold rims.

And not a piece broken. Mind you,' she added, 'it's not as if we didn't have china. My bridesmaid's buying me a set. And we're well off for furniture. I'm to get my mother's dresser, and we're saving up for fireside chairs. Of course, my lad's earning a good wage now.'

'Ssh, Jess.' Katy, one of the girls, nudged her, noticing Bet's face.

But Jess took no notice. 'Aye, he's likely to be promoted. Of course, I'll be leaving work when I get married.'

Suddenly Bet got up and hurried outside. Behind her there was a silence.

'You're a daft gomeril, Jess,' said one of the girls. 'What makes you go on like that, knowing Bet's lad's never likely to work again?'

'Well,' Jess sniffed. 'That's hardly my fault, is it? And the world has to go on.'

'You're heartless,' said another. 'How do you think she feels, you going on about weddings and presents and all that when her lad's not able to support her?'

'Oh … well…' Jess now had the grace to look a little ashamed.

Alice followed Bet outside and found her leaning against the wall, the corner of her apron stuffed in her mouth.

'Take no notice of Jess,' said Alice, putting a hand on her friend's arm. 'That's just like her. She doesn't care about anybody's feelings...'

'But it's true!' Bet said in a toneless kind of voice. 'My Jackie's not going to be able to support me. He has to look after his mother, too. And where's the money going to come from?'

Alice didn't know what to say.

'So all this talk of weddings – well, it fair turns me up,' said Bet. 'Seeing as how I'm never likely to have a wedding and a show of presents, and folk giving me china and all that...

'But it's not that, not really. I wanted to have my own house, not be living with my mother and all the bairns the way I do. Oh, I know it's grand having a family but the noise and the squabbling and always being at someone's beck and call... Well, I wanted a wee place just for Jackie and me on our own. I wanted to polish my own furniture, wash and clean – and I wanted bairns of my own...' Her voice broke.

'I know it's hard. But–' Alice tried to find some words that might be consoling. 'Things will work out,' she finished lamely.

'Will they?' Bet turned on her. 'You

haven't seen him. He's a cripple, my Jackie, and always will be. So how will things work out? Just you tell me that!'

'I don't know, but...' Alice's voice faltered.

'Oh, it's all right for you. You've got skills – you've been promoted. You'll soon be earning a lot more than any of us. The rest of us – the ones like me, who can't do anything else – have worked away in the shed for years, in the dust and the heat and the freezing cold in winter, with no chance of promotion. And you come in, and in no time you're Old Frosty's favourite, and you're promoted over the rest of us.

'And your wee drawings – everyone says, "Isn't she clever?", and no doubt you are. But how do you think it looks to the rest of us, the ones who've got no skills and no luck, and have to work away day after day knowing that we're never going to get any-where? And there's hundreds, and thou-sands like us all over the country, in mills and potteries, never likely to get on.' She stopped for a moment and drew a deep breath.

'Jackie was the only good thing that ever happened to me. And I was looking forward to making a life together. Oh, I know it would have been hard, him at the fishing and me always waiting, watching for him to come home. But we'd have been together. And now...'

'I'm sorry.' Alice was shaken by her friend's words. 'I never knew you felt that way about me. I'm sorry. I didn't mean to seem as if I thought I was better than the rest of you. Because I'm not.'

'Oh, I don't suppose I really meant it,' said Bet in a tired voice. 'I'm just upset. Pay no heed to me.'

Alice desperately wanted to do something to help. 'I wish I could.'

'There's nothing anyone can do,' Bet interrupted. 'And he's broken it off. Says he'll be no good to me. If he can't provide for a wife, there's no use our getting wed. So that's it. I'll not be getting my ring after all. Or my own place, or my wedding, or my show of presents.'

She seemed for a moment as if she were about to break down, but then she drew a deep breath and wiped her eyes.

'So that's how it was,' she said. 'And now we'd better get back to work or I'll be getting my books.'

She turned and went back into the shed, while Alice stood and looked after her, with a feeling of gnawing misery inside.

Chapter Seven

Taking A Chance

'You're kind of down, lass,' Chrissie said. 'Are you off your food?'

'No, it's fine.' But Alice laid down her fork. 'It's just – I'm not very hungry.'

'I'll eat it.' Young Eck reached across the table but Chrissie slapped his hand.

'That you'll not! Haven't I brought you up proper? You should know better than taking the food off folks' plates. You need a man's hand, that's what you need.'

She turned her attention back to Alice.

'Just leave it, lass, if you're not hungry.' She paused. 'You're not – missing that lad of yours?'

'George? Oh no.' Alice smiled to herself. It hadn't taken very long for George to find someone else. Just last week she had met him again, on the way from church, smart as ever in a dark suit and stiff white collar. Beside him had been the same girl, tall, buxom, and for a moment Alice had envied the luxuriant red-gold curls that escaped under the brim of her dark blue feathered hat. But only for a moment, for as they approached, she'd heard the girl's voice. It had been loud, even strident, though George had been looking at her with great admiration.

As they passed, George had bowed rather stiffly, while the girl had looked at Alice with open curiosity.

Alice grinned. He hadn't wasted much time – but somehow she felt that the red-haired girl would be a match for George, and possibly for his mother, too.

But now, Alice refused to answer any more questions from Chrissie.

'You've not got a lad then?'

'There's time enough.' Alice wouldn't be drawn further.

'Now,' she thought, 'I've got to work, to get on, if ever I'm to be a real artist. One day, I'll prove myself to the likes of George.'

But one day was a long time ahead…

Even so, it wasn't many weeks before the overseer came up as Alice was finishing off a plate.

'Not bad,' he said approvingly. 'You're learning,' he added. 'I think we'll put you on to decorating. You can help Miss Gray.'

Once, Alice would have been overjoyed

with this praise – or what passed for praise from the overseer. But not now – now, she admitted to herself, that she was lonely. Her friendship with Bet had cooled since Bet's outburst, and they were no longer on the same comfortable terms. Now, when Alice went to join the others at break time, she could feel the coolness, almost as if Bet didn't want to know her.

'I wish there was something I could do to help,' she thought. 'But I can't even help myself, so what can I do for Bet?'

Alice was beginning to realise that she was stuck in a situation which would never improve. Oh, it was great to have been promoted to being a decorator, and the overseer was obviously satisfied with her work, but she longed to be a proper artist.

'They're good, but nothing special,' she thought, looking at her recent paintings. 'They're just nice little sketches of flowers – any lady with a modest talent for sketching in her spare time could do as well. I've got to have lessons.'

However, there was no money; every spare penny she had went on paints or drawing paper.

But then Miss Jenkins, the head cashier, called to Alice one day.

'I hear you're quite the artist.'

Alice blushed. 'Well…' she said guardedly.

'There's a lot of scrap paper here – old bills and advertisements. I was going to throw them out. Any use to you?'

'Oh, thank you!' Alice was really grateful. It would save quite a lot, she thought, being able to sketch on the back of the discarded paper.

So she was able to struggle along, sketching, painting in her spare time.

'But I need proper lessons,' she told herself. 'I'm never going to learn otherwise. And how ever am I going to pay for lessons? I might as well give up now.'

And then, as she folded her chemises one evening, she had an idea. She reached into the drawer and brought out the black leather box in which she kept the pendant Mrs Macfee had given her. She fingered the delicate gold setting and savoured the smooth feel of the amethyst…

'So you want to sell this?' The jeweller looked at Alice shrewdly.

'Yes, please. I need the money.' Alice was direct.

'It's a nice piece,' said the jeweller. 'You could – if it's of sentimental value, like – you could pawn it. Get it back when you can.'

'No. I don't like pawnbrokers.' Alice was quite firm. 'And I want the money. I'm not likely to be able to redeem it.'

'Very well.' He looked at the piece more closely. 'It's a nice piece, as I said, but not worth a lot.'

'But I thought...'

'There's not much call for semi-precious stones.' The man was more kindly now. He looked at Alice in her worn black jacket and heavy grey skirt. 'I tell you what I'll do. I'll give you the money, and I'll keep it for a bit. Maybe you'll change your mind.'

'That's what pawnbrokers do,' said Alice.

'I'm not a pawnbroker.' The man stroked his greying moustache. 'But I've a feeling your luck might change.'

'I'm not after charity,' Alice protested.

'It's not charity.' The man turned away. 'Make up your mind. I'm busy.'

The shop did not seem busy, Alice thought. In fact, she was the only customer.

'All right.'

He named a price. It was not as much as Alice had hoped. For some weeks now she had paused in front of the jewellers' windows in the High Street, gazing at rings and brooches, and had imagined she would get a tidy sum.

'It's second-hand,' the man said quickly. 'Not much call for second-hand.'

Alice put the money carefully in her purse and left the shop.

It was a few days later that she searched through the columns of the local paper. There were the usual advertisements: *Piano lessons, 10s a session; Woman wishes to take in family washing.* She skimmed over the adverts for pianos – a Challen rosewood piano for £16 – and fashions; she sighed, wishing she could afford a costume in mole-coloured Venetian cloth, with a black silk collar and black and white silk piping, for 79s 6d. But she would never be able to afford that, she thought with a sigh.

She turned back to the columns of adverts and suddenly one sprang out at her:

Painting classes. Mr James proposes starting a painting class on Saturday forenoons, for beginners. Apply...

'That's not much use to me,' thought Alice. She worked on a Saturday forenoon. 'But he might take me on privately...'

She looked again at the address. It was near the park; she knew the road and remembered the large houses.

That evening she gathered together the few paintings she had produced recently – the vivid picture of cornfield poppies; a sketch of Chrissie. 'My, that's great – it's awful like me,' Chrissie had said, gratified. And one or two sketches, less successful, of the steamers at the harbour.

The house stood out among those in the street. For a start the windows badly needed cleaning, and the paint on the front door was clipped. The garden, too, in comparison with the neat stretches of gravel bordering the houses on either side, looked neglected, as if someone with great enthusiasm had once tried to make a cottage garden and had given up, discouraged.

Her paintings firmly clutched under one arm, Alice rang the bell – a brass bell, she noticed, that had not been polished in many a year.

'Yes?' The tall man who stood before her might have been any age, stooped, with grizzled hair and moustache. His manner was brisk and dismissive. 'We don't buy at the door.'

'I'm not here to sell anything.' Alice stood her ground. 'You're the man that gives painting lessons?'

'I am an artist, yes,' the man admitted. 'I

teach schools and evening classes…'

'I know.' Alice had asked Miss Lennox.

'Yes,' her former teacher had said, 'he's good. Not a top rank artist himself – but a good teacher.'

Now Alice quickly explained – where she worked, why she couldn't attend Saturday morning classes.

'You'd better come in.'

He led her into a large room with the traditional high ceiling and bow windows. Alice could see no sign of an easel or any painting and glanced around a little nervously. Had she come to the right place?

'My studio is upstairs,' he explained, seeing her discomfiture. 'More light. Now – is this your work?'

He skimmed through Alice's paintings, pausing at the picture of the poppies.

'Hmm… Mmmm… Yes…'

Alice's hopes began to rise.

'I have money to pay for lessons,' she said.

'Of course,' he said brusquely. 'I'm not a charity.'

'But you'll maybe think I'm not good enough to teach,' said Alice a little timidly. 'I don't know if I've any talent. That's what I want to find out.' She looked at him enquiringly.

'You've a lot to learn.' He tapped the paintings with, she noticed, short stubby fingers. He didn't look like an artist, she thought. She'd expected someone more ... Bohemian – maybe in a paint-stained smock. This man in a suit – a rather shabby suit – and wearing a monocle did not look like her idea of an artist. But she remembered what Miss Lennox had said.

'However,' he went on, 'I can teach you. You've a lot to learn about perspective, shading – but you've a good sense of colour. You're a decorator at Simpson's, you said? Ah, well, you'll learn a lot there.'

'So you'll teach me?'

'Yes.' Mr James put Alice's paintings neatly together. 'Now, let me see – we'll talk about times for your lessons, and terms...'

Alice's spirits rose. She was just at the beginning, but she would, she was determined, learn to be an artist.

'My dear! So this is your new pupil – Alice, isn't it?' The bell-like voice rang from the doorway and Alice turned round.

'You're interrupting us, Rebecca,' said Mr James testily.

The figure in the doorway took no notice. Alice had never seen anyone like her before. She was wearing a long, flowing garment like a kimono, patterned in a design of brilliant blue peacocks. Round her head was a bandeau of a vivid green. The woman herself had strong features, a beaky nose and a wide mouth, and might have been anything between forty and fifty. But it was not her face that impressed Alice, it was the deep, musical voice.

You'd think she was in a concert hall instead of a small room, thought Alice, trying not to giggle as the woman went on speaking, ignoring her husband.

Mrs James was not a bit put out by her husband's discouraging attitude. She advanced into the room and looked closely at Alice.

'What a face!' she said. 'How I'd like to paint that face! The cheekbones – the brow. You will let me paint you, won't you, my dear?'

Alice did not know what to say.

'My wife paints portraits,' said Mr James irritably.

'I like,' said Mrs James confidingly, 'to capture the soul of my sitter. That is so important, don't you think?'

Again Alice was not sure what to say.

'I don't know,' she murmured. 'I'm just

learning. I don't know much.'

The woman took a step back, and flung her arms out wide.

'What humility!' she cried, raising her eyes to the ceiling as if she were appealing to a higher power. 'Oh, what humility, what simplicity! I must paint you, I really must!'

'Oh, do go away, Rebecca,' said Mr James, losing patience. 'Can't you see you're interrupting a lesson?'

'Oh, very well.' Mrs James turned to go. 'But, my dear, you must see my studio and we will decide when you can come and sit for me.'

She slammed the door behind her and the pictures on the wall shook.

'Aye, well, maybe we can get on now,' said Mr James. 'I was asking you, what do you see when you look at that vase?'

Alice hesitated.

'It's different colours – dark on that side and lighter on the other.'

'And if I place it here...' He picked up the glass vase and put it on a table where a shaft of light fell through the window.

Alice couldn't help noticing that the windows had not been cleaned for a very long time and the sunlight obviously struggled to battle through the grime. Clearly, whatever sort of painter Mrs James might be, house-work was not one of her accomplishments.

'It's quite different,' said Alice.

'Good...' said her teacher. 'You're beginning to notice.'

After that she was concentrating so hard that she had little time to think about Mrs James, but as she left, she could hear someone singing in a strong contralto, loudly but not very tunefully.

She looked back at the house as she walked down the path to the gate. There were a few marigolds and some stocks in the border, but mostly the ground was choked with weeds. Alice automatically pulled out a few pieces of the weed she knew as sticky willie. That was what the orphans had called it. She remembered how, on trips to the countryside, they'd look for the weed and stick it to the back of an unsuspecting friend.

'Well,' she thought, 'I'm learning. But I'd like to see her paintings. I've never met a real artist before.'

'So, how did you get on with Mr James?' Miss Lennox asked as she poured tea from the old silver teapot and handed the cup to Alice.

'He seems to be a very good teacher.'

Miss Lennox nodded approvingly. 'I thought you'd learn a lot from him.'

'I'm just at the beginning,' said Alice hastily. 'I've a lot to learn. I didn't know how much.' For a moment she looked a bit downcast.

'Don't worry,' Miss Lennox reassured her. 'You *know* you've a lot to learn, and that's half the battle. It's the ones who think they already know everything who are never likely to amount to anything.'

She passed over a plate of scones. 'And how are you getting on at work?'

Alice hesitated.

'Mr McCracken says I'm improving.'

'That's high praise from him,' said her old teacher with a smile. 'He doesn't offer praise easily.'

Alice wondered if she should tell Miss Lennox about the tensions between her and the other girls. Then she decided not to. It wouldn't solve anything, and it was her problem, and hers alone.

But she couldn't help feeling miserable whenever Bet walked past without her usual cheerful good morning, and deliberately sat some way apart from her at the morning break. It had been such a good friendship, and there was little Alice could do to repair it. But poor Bet – she looked so unhappy. Nowadays she didn't speak about the dances or the plans for her wedding. Would she and her Jackie ever get married? Or was Jackie too proud and stubborn, knowing that he couldn't provide for a wife?

'Yes, it's all right,' she said to Miss Lennox, pushing the thoughts of Bet to the back of her mind. 'In fact, I've got something for you. Mr McCracken let me buy it, seeing as it was the first I'd done. Not the very first, mind,' she added hastily. 'That was all wrong and smudged.'

She grimaced, remembering the overseer's shout of rage that 'a two-year-old could do better!'

She handed the brown paper parcel to Miss Lennox.

'For me?' Her teacher looked surprised.

'A thank you,' said Alice. 'You've been very good to me.'

Carefully Miss Lennox opened the parcel and gave a gasp of pleasure.

'It's beautiful.'

'No, it's not,' said Alice honestly. 'I've a lot to learn. But I wanted you to have the first good one.'

Miss Lennox traced with her fingers the pattern of the blowsy pink cabbage roses, and the delicate shades of green of the leaves.

'I will treasure this,' she said, as she placed the plate on the shelf. 'Thank you, my dear.'

Chapter Eight

A Tall, Dark Stranger

'This can't go on,' said Alice to herself, as Bet rose very pointedly and moved away from her to sit next to Jess.

Jess, of all people! Alice remembered how often Bet had laughed at Jess, at her airs and graces. And now they seemed to be the best of friends, sitting with their heads close together.

'What have I done?' thought Alice. 'She thought I was getting above myself, but I'm not – I'm just the same person.

'Well, not quite the same,' she added truthfully. Since Rebecca and her husband had started to take an interest in her she was learning quickly, not just about painting and drawing but about a world which she had never dreamed she could enter, a world where people read books, and talked about politics and art, and argued without falling out with one another. It was a world she had never known existed.

But Bet – why couldn't she be friends with Bet as well?

At the end of the day when the bell went for stopping time, the girls gathered up their jackets and piece tins and hurried out of the gate as quickly as they could.

Bet followed rather more slowly, and Alice ran to catch her up.

'Bet – wait a minute!'

Bet turned round and was about to walk on quickly, but Alice grabbed her by the arm.

'Don't rush off. I want to talk to you. Please, can we not be friends again? I don't know what I've done to offend you, but I didn't mean it, honest.'

Bet looked at her for a moment. 'Och, you don't want to be bothered with the likes of me.'

She started to walk on again, but Alice caught her up.

'Can you not tell me what the matter is? After all,' she went on, a little breathlessly, 'we've been good chums in the past.'

'That was the past,' said Bet stiffly, 'and

this is now. So that's all there is to be said. You'll not want to be troubled with the likes of me, you with your grand new friends.'

'Grand new friends?' Alice laughed, and then she saw that Bet was perfectly serious. 'You can't mean Mr James and his wife? He's teaching me to draw, that's all. I'm never likely to be close friends with them. They're – they're not my class.'

'You visit their house,' Bet pointed out.

'For drawing lessons, that's all. Not as a friend or a visitor,' Alice insisted.

'Oh, well...' Bet was not entirely convinced.

'That's not like you,' said Alice. 'You'd never have minded before who I saw or who I visited...'

'That was before,' Bet said. 'Anyway, I wish you luck. You've got everything you want...'

'Oh, Bet,' said Alice, 'I wish you could see – I'm still the same person.'

Bet looked at the honest, troubled face of her friend, and all her misery suddenly spilled out.

'I suppose I'm jealous of you,' she said. 'You've got everything. You've been promoted to a good job. You don't need to work in that dusty shed. What do you think it's like, year in, year out, doing the same old thing day after day? And when you come down at break time, it's like you weren't one of us – as if you were slumming…'

'Bet!' Alice protested hotly. 'I would never be like that. I come for the company. It's kind of lonely, working alone except for Miss Gray.'

'Oh, all right,' said Bet shrugging her shoulders. 'I knew you wouldn't be a snob, really…'

'Come on, Bet,' Alice urged. 'We've been good pals. I miss the laughs we had…'

'Me, too,' said Bet. 'But that's in the past. Things have changed.'

'I know,' said Alice. 'It's been hard for you, with Jackie's accident.' She paused, not knowing quite what to say. 'But he's getting on, isn't he?'

'He'll never be able to go back to the fishing,' said Bet tonelessly. 'He says there's nothing to look forward to. And–' she gave a little sob '–and he's quite determined. He doesn't want to marry me now.'

'Oh, Bet.' Alice stopped, silent now. After a moment, she said, 'But you were to be married quite soon.'

'That was before. Now he says he'll never be able to support me. And he's proud –

they all are, the fisher people. And if he can't support me, he won't marry me. And that's all there is to it.

'So you see,' she went on, 'when everyone's sitting laughing and joking at break time about lads and weddings and that, and there's you with your job and being a real decorator – maybe I'm being mean and grudging, but I can't see any future for me. That's why I don't care, why I'm not very friendly. Because I haven't got Jackie, so I've nothing to look forward to, nothing at all.'

'Your new pupil is a talented child,' said Rebecca James to her husband.

'She's doing well,' he admitted. 'She has a lot to learn, but she's a trier.'

'Poor girl,' said Rebecca thoughtfully. 'So thin, so shabby – and working in a pottery.' She shuddered. 'All that dust... I think she has refinement, that girl. Something could be made of her.'

'You are not to interfere,' said her husband sternly. 'I forbid you.'

Rebecca smiled in the way he knew very well. It meant she had heard him but still she was determined to have her own way in the end.

'I wouldn't dream of interfering,' she said

sweetly. 'But she needs someone to help her.'

'She's got Miss Lennox, her old teacher. She's a good sort.'

'Oh, Miss Lennox.' Rebecca gave a theatrical shudder. 'I wouldn't trust her to teach refinement to anyone. I believe,' she said with an air of distaste, 'she is one of those what-do-you-call-them – suffragettes. Those women who want the vote. I've heard she goes to meetings, and speaks up for women's suffrage.'

'And why not?' said Frederick James sharply. 'She's got a good head on her shoulders, a lot of common sense. She's a good example to young Alice.'

'Surely–' Rebecca traced her finger in the dust on the piano lid and absently thought, I must do something about this. 'Surely no woman could be in favour of the vote? We don't need it. We are perfectly capable of ordering our own lives – and those of our husbands,' she added with a smile. 'Anyway,' she said, 'I live for my art. I have more important things to think of.'

Her husband sighed. They had had this argument many times before. Just for once, he wished that Rebecca would put on a pinafore like other wives and do a bit of dusting and tidying up. But, he reproached himself, he had not married her as a housewife, he had married this vibrant, artistic personality. And she was good-hearted, he admitted. If only...

'I think it's time we gave one of my soirées,' said Rebecca. 'Nothing grand. Perhaps just tea and my elderflower cordial, and fruit cake – and music. Maybe dancing – we could ask Bobby Lawson, he plays most beautifully. Yes, a little music in the background, and conversation – it's the conversation that's most important.

'There is so little conversation in this town,' she added. 'People can only talk about the price of food, and getting a reliable woman to do the washing, and that kind of thing. So few are interested in art. And–' she suddenly had a bright idea '–I will ask your little protégée. It will introduce her into society.'

'Humph...' was all Frederick James said. He knew better than to interrupt Rebecca when she was in hot pursuit of a new idea, but his heart sank. A soirée indeed! Where did she get these mad ideas?

A week later, when Alice had nearly finished her lesson, the door opened.

'Are you busy?' trilled Rebecca.

'Yes,' said her husband. 'What do you want, Rebecca?'

'I want Alice, when you've finished the lesson. Come upstairs, my dear. I shall be in my sitting-room.'

After the lesson, Frederick said to Alice. 'You're making progress. Now, go on, my wife's got some ploy or other. You'd better humour her. Upstairs, first door on the right,' he urged.

In the workroom, Rebecca was surrounded by lengths of cloth and brilliantly coloured skirts and blouses, some of them delicate lawn, others of striped silk, or creamy linen trimmed with lace.

'Come in, my dear. Now, you are going to be at my little soirée, aren't you?'

Alice did not quite know what to say.

'It's very kind of you…' It was the sort of occasion she had dreamed of; artists, writers, musicians – she had never before had a chance to talk to people like that. Not that she would be talking. But just to listen, to hear such brilliant conversation. It would be a wonderful opportunity.

'I know what you're going to say,' Rebecca told her kindly. 'You're going to say, "I can't come because I've nothing to wear," aren't

160

you? But here is the answer.' Rebecca waved her arm at the dresses and material surrounding her. 'I have lots of clothes which would be suitable, and I'm sure we can find something becoming. Take off your skirt and your blouse.'

Alice, feeling a little shy, stood in her chemise while Rebecca handed her a long skirt in bright scarlet.

'That, I think – and a blouse ... black, or white – and you'll need something vivid, bright red, or orange, for the scarf...' She draped a scarf round Alice's head and a headband covered with bright feathers, with a scarf attached.

'There – you look quite different.' Rebecca gazed approvingly at the girl. 'Go on, look in the mirror.'

Alice stared aghast at the stranger in the glass. Her rosy face and auburn curls looked quite incongruous in the bright finery.

'I should be a dark gypsy-looking type,' she thought.

'What is it? You don't seem absolutely thrilled, my dear. Shall we try something else? Perhaps all black with a dramatic peacock blue scarf?'

About half an hour later, Alice was beginning to run out of excuses.

'It's most kind of you,' she said, 'but they're not... I mean, I don't really suit any of the clothes. They're for someone grander than me...'

'Well, my dear,' said Rebecca. 'If you change your mind, you know I have a large wardrobe... Now I wonder – perhaps creamy lace would be more your style.'

'Oh, please,' Alice protested, 'you've been kind enough to me. I can't take up more of your time.'

'Very well,' said Rebecca agreeably. 'But if you change your mind.'

'Perhaps I've made a mistake,' Alice thought as she lifted from the rail her good navy skirt and freshly starched white cotton blouse. 'Maybe I should have taken up Rebecca's offer. She meant it kindly. But I'd have felt like someone dressed up for a play, not really me.'

She began to doubt, too, whether she had been wise to accept the invitation to the soirée. She had never been to a soirée before. Did one wear gloves? Or a hat? And what would she have to say to these people – artists, some of them, all well educated? People who knew about paintings and music and books...

She gave herself a little shake.

'Rebecca was being thoughtful, asking me. It would be rude to turn down the invitation.'

All the same as she made her way along the pavements towards the Jameses' house, she couldn't help feeling apprehensive.

'There you are, my dear!' As Rebecca folded her in a warm hug, Alice felt uncomfortable. Where she came from acquaintances didn't hug each other – and neither did families, very much.

'I thought you'd changed your mind. Now come in and have a glass of my elderflower cordial. Or maybe lemonade? And there are so many people I want you to meet.'

She was introduced to a stout lady in grey silk. 'Mrs McKay – this is Alice, my husband's young protégée. She's a very talented artist, you know.'

'Oh, Rebecca,' thought Alice, 'I wish you wouldn't!'

But the lady in grey turned out to be not at all alarming. It appeared that she had been a neighbour of the Jameses, and had looked after Rebecca when she had influenza.

'We were fair worried about her,' she confided. 'Her temperature was away up and there was nothing the doctor could do. "I'll

163

have to leave it to you, Mrs McKay," he said. "It's only nursing will pull her through." And it did. I was a nurse before I married, you see, so I'd seen lots of cases.'

Instantly Alice felt reassured by this homely, comfortable woman and a style of conversation she was accustomed to.

'So where do you live, lass?' asked Mrs McKay.

In a few minutes, she had extracted most of Alice's history. Usually Alice didn't like talking about the orphanage, but she found herself chatting quite naturally to the woman, who listened sympathetically.

'I know the matron – a kind body, but strict.'

'Yes, she was, but…'

'Aye,' said Mrs McKay. 'Now you'll not want to spend the entire time talking to an old body like me. My nephew's here – he brought me – he'll be more your age. Alec!' she called across the room. 'I'm no' very sure why they asked me there's a lot of right clever folk here. But that's Rebecca – a warm heart, she has.'

A young man, somewhere in his twenties, with a mop of untidy fair hair, crossed the room.

'Now you take care of this lassie,' Mrs Mc-

Kay told him. 'She'll not know many folk here.'

'Right you are, Auntie,' said the young man obligingly. 'There's going to be dancing in a minute. My chum, Bobby, plays the piano. Do you dance, Miss Finlay?'

'A little,' said Alice, hesitating. She recalled the eightsomes and the Lancers at the fishermen's dances. There wasn't likely to be anything as wild or uncontrolled here, but the floor had been cleared, and the pianist struck up a waltz.

'Will you dance?' said Alec.

'Thank you.'

He steered her expertly through the waltz. The room was crowded and one or two ladies had brought out elaborate fans. Rebecca herself was waltzing serenely with another young man.

Then the tempo changed.

'Oh,' said Alec, 'you'll know the two-step. This is the latest one, Billy Possum's Frolic.'

'What a comical name!' Alice found herself laughing.

'It's the hit of the moment,' said the young man. 'Come on, let's try it.'

Alice discovered that it wasn't as hard as she'd imagined, and Alec led her expertly through the steps.

'You're a natural,' he said approvingly. 'Do you dance a lot?'

Alice, breathless, shook her head.

'You should…'

She turned swiftly and stumbled against a tall man who was watching the dancing. The drink he was holding spilt, and Alice stopped, aghast.

'I'm terribly sorry.'

'No matter.' He mopped at the front of his suit with an immaculate white handkerchief.

'It was clumsy of me.'

'Not at all,' he said. 'You were dancing very well, I thought. Most accomplished.'

The music stopped and Alec waited, a little uncertain.

'I'm going to take this young lady from you,' the man told him, 'and she will have the next dance with me. But first I will find her a glass of lemonade. I'm sure you must be thirsty after all that dancing,' he said to Alice.

Unsure, Alice turned to Alec.

'That's all right,' he said easily. 'We'll have a waltz later on.'

The tall man grasped Alice by the arm. She glanced up at him – a sharp, almost beaky nose and a half-amused expression.

She said, a little stiffly, 'I do apologise.'

'No need to keep apologising. I would ask you to dance, but I'm afraid I don't dance…'

Alice must have looked a little taken aback for he said, 'It's my turn to apologise. I have taken you away from your partner under false pretences. But I wanted to talk to you… Now, may I fetch you lemonade, or a glass of our hostess's elderflower cordial?'

'Lemonade, please.'

He gave her a look, as if they shared a confidence. 'Perhaps you're wise.'

'And now,' he said as he returned, 'let us sit down. I think there is to be musical entertainment.' He found her a chair.

'I haven't seen you at the Jameses' soirées before. Are you a painter?' he asked.

Alice shook her head. 'But I'm learning. I'm studying with Frederick – Mr James.'

'An excellent teacher: you will learn a great deal from him,' he said approvingly.

Alice was too shy to ask what he did for a living. The suit on which she had splashed the drink was a pale grey and his shirt and collar were spotlessly clean. He was some years older than Alice – perhaps in his early thirties, and, she thought, spoke confidently as if he knew his way about. For a moment she regretted that she had not kept to the company of the cheerful, uncomplicated Alec.

'So where do you work?' he asked.

'At Simpson's – the pottery.'

'I know them. A good firm to be with.'

In no time, Alice found herself telling him how she had started at Simpson's, about her promotion to being a decorator, and, a little shyly, about her ambition to be an artist.

He listened as if he were really interested, and she found he knew a good deal about art and artists. He could tell her about the galleries he had visited and which painters she should look out for.

'You haven't told me your name,' he said.

'Ssh…' said someone behind them. 'Mrs James is going to play.'

Rebecca sat down at the piano, lifted her hands above the keyboard, and waved her fingers at the audience. Then she began playing a Chopin Prelude. Everyone listened attentively, though it was clear she made one or two mistakes, and when she finished with a triumphant flourish the applause was genuinely warm.

'Encore!' someone cried.

'If you must,' she said, and launched willingly into a waltz.

Someone behind Alice and her new friend

said, in a voice that was not meant to be heard, 'Our hostess is as amateur a pianist as she is a painter.'

Alice's companion turned round and fixed the young man with a glare.

'And an accomplished hostess,' he said, 'even towards guests with unforgiveably boorish manners.'

The young man flushed and looked embarrassed.

Rebecca got up gracefully from the piano stool and gave a little bow.

'Now someone else must play,' she insisted, and the cheerful, red-haired man who had played for the dancing took her place.

'Selections from Our Miss Gibbs,' he announced, to a round of applause.

'Splendid! The very latest!' said someone approvingly next to Alice.

Oh, thought Alice, this was turning out to be much more enjoyable than she had expected.

'Perhaps you'd like to dance again. I don't want to keep you from your partners,' Alice's companion said, but she shook her head.

'I don't really care.'

'Then let's sit down. Perhaps we can find somewhere quiet.'

But at that moment, Rebecca swooped down on them.

'Ah, I see you've captured our little friend,' she said to the tall man. 'Now, there is someone who is longing to talk to you, so I'm going to take you away. And, come along, my dear – Alec is anxious to dance with you again.'

'But...' the man protested, but Rebecca wasn't listening.

'I have enjoyed talking to you,' he said, with a little bow. 'I wish you good luck in your studies with Frederick.'

Alec appeared at Alice's elbow. 'Would you like to dance this one with me? It's a waltz.'

Wistfully Alice looked after the tall, dark man who Rebecca was marching towards a group in the far corner.

She did not see him again, but thought of their conversation as she was escorted home by Alec.

'Well, that was a jolly evening,' he said. 'Some artists, some musicians – a good mixture, I'd say. And the children of friends. They don't have children of their own, Frederick and Rebecca, and they like having young people around, feeding them, giving them a good time.'

'I enjoyed it,' said Alice.

'Good.' The young man paused. 'Is this where you live?'

Alice nodded, and waited for him to retreat quickly.

But, 'Maybe we could go out one evening? A concert, perhaps, or a show at the Palace Theatre?'

'Yes, thank you,' said Alice, a little absently, for she was still thinking of the tall, dark man. Who was he? She was determined to find out...

Chapter Nine

Bet's Bright Idea

It was such a different world, thought Alice next morning as she picked up her brush and began working on a violet-patterned plate. To have been talking, dancing, mixing with a group of people she would never normally have met. People who had no idea what it was like to grow up in an orphanage, to have no family. To struggle to make ends meet. To think twice before you could buy a new pair of gloves.

'Stop feeling sorry for yourself,' she told herself briskly. She was lucky, she knew, to have the chance to meet artists – real artists. 'It might lead to something,' she thought.

'Miss Finlay...?' Miss Gray had already called across to Alice.

Alice brought her thoughts back to the present. 'I'm sorry – I didn't hear you.'

'It's a special order,' said Miss Gray. 'For a wedding gift, I understand. They've asked for a complete dressing-table set – the wild rose pattern. I'm going to be pretty busy,' she added, 'what with the bowl to finish.' Alice knew Miss Gray was working on a presentation bowl for the retirement presentation to a local councillor and his wife.

'Do you think you could handle this?'

'Aye, you can manage that.' Mr Mc-Cracken spoke behind them. They had not heard him come up the stair.

He looked on approvingly. 'We've a fair lot of work on hand,' he said proudly. 'I've been thinking – och, well, you'll both find a bit more in your pay packets next Friday.' And he was gone down the stairs before they could thank him.

Miss Gray looked across at Alice. 'Well, that'll come in handy, I must say.'

'He's–' Alice hesitated. 'He's in a much

better temper these days.'

'Oh, that's because of the son. You'll know the boy? He's studying to be a doctor, at the university in Edinburgh. His father's like a cat with two tails. He can't see past that laddie. Mind you, he's a nice lad. Not so wild as he was.'

'They've only the one?' Alice wasn't minded to gossip, but she had met Mr McCracken's son and liked the cheerful, good-natured young man who was not above joking with the men who fired the pots.

'Just the one. No wonder he's the apple of his father's eye. And speaking of fruit–' Miss Gray picked up the pot she'd been working on, a small jam pot with a pattern of cherries. 'I like this pattern. It's cheery. It's a piece I wouldn't mind having myself.'

At break time Alice went down to join the others, and determinedly crossed the room to sit beside Bet. Bet looked up but didn't say anything.

'How are you getting on?' Alice asked.

Bet shrugged and said nothing.

'I thought,' Alice ploughed on, 'if you're not going out with Jackie, maybe we could go for a walk on Saturday afternoon. Maybe take a look at the shops...' She paused expecting Bet to refuse.

'All right,' Bet said tonelessly.

'That's fine then.' Alice didn't say any more.

So on Saturday afternoon, Alice and Bet met up at the corner of the street.

'Let's have a look at the shop windows in the High Street,' said Alice cheerfully.

'I'll not be able to afford to buy anything,' said Bet.

'I know,' said Alice. 'I can't either, come to that. But we can look, and decide what we would buy if we were rich.'

Bet nodded. She didn't seem the least bit interested, thought Alice, remembering what her friend had once been like.

Alice kept up her monologue all the way along the High Street.

'Now there's a hat I could wear,' she said, pointing to a large navy blue straw trimmed with flowers. 'And look at these gloves – real kid.'

But Bet did not seem much interested.

'We could have a cup of tea,' Alice suggested at last. 'I'll treat you.'

Sitting in the teashop, Bet's spirits began to revive.

'It's that Jess that gets on my nerves,' she said suddenly. 'With her talk of weddings and show of presents and bouquets and such. I could slap her sometimes, I could.'

Alice nodded sympathetically.

'*You're* not like that,' said Bet suddenly.

'I haven't got a lad,' said Alice, 'so I've no call to start boasting.'

'Oh, you'll maybe find someone – what about that George you were walking out with?'

'That's all finished,' said Alice firmly. 'He's got someone else now.'

'He was really proper,' said Bet a little enviously.

'Too proper.' Alice shook her head. 'I like a lad who likes a bit of a laugh from time to time. Like...' She stopped herself in time.

'You were going to say, like Jackie...'

Alice reached across the table and grasped her friend's hand.

'Cheer up. He's getting better, you said so yourself.'

Bet sighed. 'But the thing is, he's that proud. We were going to be wed, he was going to buy me a ring. But now he says he won't marry me because he can't support a wife.' She fished a handkerchief out of her sleeve and wiped her eyes. 'As if I minded! I'd sooner be poor with Jackie than rich with anyone else.'

'Is there nothing he could do?'

Bet shrugged. 'He'll not be back at the fishing – he'll not be fit enough. And it's heavy work in the linoleum works or in the pottery. He said–' she gave a gulp '–he said he wouldn't hold me to my promise. I could go and find someone else, but I don't want anyone else. I want Jackie.' Her voice rose to a wail.

'I've said,' she went on, 'that I'll wait for him, but it's hard...' She put her handkerchief away. 'What about you? You're getting lessons from that Mr James.'

Alice nodded. She wondered if she should tell Bet about the soirée. At one time they would have shared everything, but now...

'Come on,' she said, 'we'd better be moving.'

The two girls came out of the shop into the bright sunshine, and turned up a little side street. There were children playing in the street, and a boy bouncing a ball against a wall.

'I've just remembered,' said Bet suddenly. 'I promised to buy some pan drops for my mother. They're her favourite.'

'We'll look out for a sweetie shop then,' said Alice.

They found a shop not far from Coal Row. A couple of ragged urchins had their noses

176

pressed against the window. Inside, an old woman, a shawl round her head, sat knitting a sock.

'What do ye want?' she said, glowering at the girls.

'Pan drops – a quarter, please,' said Bet, looking round at the shop, at the cobwebs in the corners, the jars of sweets and sticks of rock, the toffee twists and peppermints, and black and white striped balls. It looked as if the old woman had never cleaned the windows or swept the floor.

'Have you been here a long time?' she asked suddenly.

'I have that.' The woman looked at her suspiciously. 'But not much longer,' she added. 'I'm going to live with my daughter and her man in Buckhaven. And I'll be glad to be out of this place, I can tell you. They've been at me for a while now. "Come and stay with us, Mother. You'll be a help with the bairns".'

The girls found it hard to believe that anyone would really want this cantankerous old woman to live with them, and felt a moment's pity for the lively children who would be sharing a home with her.

'So,' said Alice politely, 'what will happen to the shop? Who will take it over?'

'You're a one to spier,' said the woman, again suspiciously. 'That's up to the land-lord. I'm not bothered, to tell you the truth. I've worked my fingers to the bone here, and never a thank you.'

Alice thought there was little evidence of anyone working their fingers to the bone. A gloomier, more depressing shop she had seldom seen. But then, it was the only sweet shop for some distance, and she supposed there were occasional customers.

Bet paid for her pan drops and said politely, 'I hope you'll be happy with your daughter and family.'

'It's not likely,' said the woman. 'But I'll be useful anyway. Now see and steek the door properly when you go out,' she told them. 'I'm not wanting any of these wild laddies in here,' she said, and returned to her knitting.

Outside Alice drew a deep breath.

'My, you'd need to be brave to go in there,' she said. The two girls started giggling, and suddenly it was like old times again. Bet laughed until she was gasping, holding her sides.

'Here,' she said, offering the bag to Alice, 'have a pan drop,' and that set them off laughing again.

Alice put a hand on her friend's arm. 'Keep

smiling,' she said. 'Things will get better, I know they will.'

'I hope so,' said Bet soberly now. 'Because if they don't, I'm not sure what we'll do, Jackie and me.'

But there was something else on Alice's mind. She had enjoyed the soirée at the Jameses much more than she had expected. And the best part had been meeting the tall man with the dark hair and the half smile. It was a very long time since she had met anyone like him. 'No, be truthful,' she told herself, 'you have *never* met anyone like him.'

She remembered the way he had smiled at her, the way he had listened to her and made her feel – well, like someone worth listening to. It had all been going so well, and then he had simply disappeared.

'I don't know his name or anything about him,' she thought. 'And anyway, he wouldn't seek me out. I'm just a girl who works in a pottery. Even though I am a decorator, I'm not like any of the Jameses' friends. Why should he bother with the likes of me?'

Still, she felt that little nagging ache of misery and loss. How pleasant it would have been if he'd said he enjoyed talking to her, or – her imagination caught fire – if he'd said, 'Now that I've found you, I must see you again.'

'Alice, you're not concentrating.' Frederick James broke into her reverie. 'You're wasting your time and mine.'

'I'm sorry,' said Alice, returning to the present. After the lesson, she thought, she would ask Rebecca – tactfully, of course – about the stranger.

'It was a lovely evening,' she said, 'and very kind of you to invite me.'

'My dear, it was a pleasure,' said Rebecca. 'We like having young people around – even those silly nephews and their passion for the latest popular songs. Meaningless, most of them. But, they're young.'

'I met so many very interesting people,' Alice ploughed on.

'I'm glad you enjoyed it,' said Rebecca. 'You must come to my next evening.'

'There was–' Alice knew it was now or ever '–a very pleasant man who talked to me about painting. Tall, dark-haired, a sharp nose...'

'Oh, yes,' said Rebecca vaguely. 'Oh, my dear, I've no idea who he was. An artist, I think.'

Alice felt her heart sink. 'So you didn't invite him as one of your guests?' She tried to sound casual.

'Oh, he was perfectly reputable – he came with my friends the Jardines. I gather he was visiting them from Edinburgh. They did introduce him, but you know how it is – I heard his name, and I've completely forgotten. I'm stupid about names.' She looked sideways at Alice. 'You found him interesting?'

'To talk to,' said Alice hastily. 'It's a new experience for me to meet artists.'

'Well, we must see that you meet some more, and perhaps we could take you to an exhibition in Glasgow some time. You've not been to an art gallery?'

Alice shook her head.

'My dear,' said Rebecca, 'your education is just beginning.'

As she walked home that night, Alice felt despondent.

'If he's an artist in Edinburgh, he's probably mixing with all kinds of exciting people. He wouldn't give me another thought. So I should forget him,' she told herself sternly. 'If he wants to find me, he can. But he won't.'

Turning up the side street on her way back to Chrissie's, she tried to think of other things – of Bet, who was still hopeful that

Jackie might have some kind of future job. And that they might, one day, be able to marry.

Things had changed so quickly for Bet, thought Alice sadly. At one time she had been cheerful, outward-looking, happily planning her wedding. And now – it was not like Bet to turn to someone else. She was the most loyal of friends, and would be faithful to Jackie always. He was lucky to have her, she thought sombrely.

'I don't know what I'm going to do with that laddie,' said Chrissie. 'He's beyond me.' She sighed. 'It's easy for a lad of his age to get into bad company, hanging about with boys older than him.'

Alice didn't quite know what to say. She'd seen Eck at the corner of the street with a group of much older lads, a couple of them, she knew, from a family with a bad reputation.

'He'll go in the mill when he leaves school this year,' said Chrissie grimly. 'That'll settle him down.'

But Eck refused. 'I'm going to the fishing,' he said firmly.

There was many an argument between Eck and his mother. Eck would stamp out of the house in a sullen silence, with Chrissie calling behind him, 'You've not touched your tea.'

'A waste of good food,' she would complain crossly. 'Och, well, he can just do without.'

Alice was becoming tired of the constant battles, the silences, Chrissie's complaints about her son. It was a little wearying, she thought, though she understood why Chrissie was so anxious.

But she herself had other things to think about. She was concerned about Bet and her Jackie, and how hopeless the future seemed for them.

One day at break time, Bet said, 'Come outside a moment.'

They leaned against the wall in the early autumn sunshine, and Bet said casually, 'Are you doing anything on Saturday?' Saturday was to be a day off. Usually the workers at the pottery stopped at noon, but the whole works was to be closed for an outing to Perth for anyone who wanted to go. Alice had decided not to go, and Bet was reluctant to leave Jackie all day.

Alice shook her head. 'I've nothing planned.'

'Maybe we could go for a walk, take a look at the shops?'

'I've no money to spare,' said Alice.

'Nor me,' said Bet, 'but we could just look in the windows – plan what we'd buy if we had a lot of money. Like we did before. That was fun.'

Alice was pleased to see her friend looking more cheerful. 'Right. Saturday morning.'

The two girls strolled down the High Street, arm-in-arm, stopping to look at scarves and gloves and elegant shoes.

'Just imagine,' said Bet, 'having enough money to buy anything you wanted. I'd fancy a silk dress with a long train, and a feather headdress...'

'And a fan made of white lace...'

'And look at these.' Bet pointed to a pair of white kid slippers. 'Just fancy going to an evening do – a dinner maybe, with dancing afterwards. I've never been to an evening party, have you?'

Alice hesitated. She hadn't told anyone of her invitation to the Jameses soirée, it would sound too much like boasting. In any case, she wasn't likely to be invited to another, not in the near future, anyway.

'I did go to an evening at my art teacher's, but I didn't have an evening gown ... and most people weren't dressed up anyway.'

'Oh,' Bet looked a little disappointed, and Alice wondered if she should mention that Rebecca had offered her the loan of a dress. If it had been Bet, she wouldn't have hesitated to accept the borrowed outfit.

The two girls wandered up and down, choosing dresses they would like to wear, and presents for friends and family– 'If we had the money,' they always reminded themselves.

Then suddenly Bet said, 'Let's go back now. I promised Jackie I'd be along this afternoon. I'll take him some sweets from that wee sweet shop with that funny old body. It's just down here…'

Inside, the old woman was sitting on the upright chair by the counter, just as she had been the last time the two girls called.

'What are you wanting?' she said and Alice began to giggle.

'Some sweeties,' said Bet wildly, looking around.

'Aye, you've come to the right place,' said the old woman. She turned sharply to Alice. 'And what have you got to laugh about?'

With a big effort, Alice became serious. 'Me? Oh, nothing, really.'

'I'll take some taffy twist,' said Bet, and then she added, very casually, 'You told us you were giving up the shop.'

'I am that. I'll be gone come the term.'

'And you said you didn't know who was taking it over.'

'It's no business of mine,' said the old woman. 'It's all in the hands of the lawyer.'

'And who might that be?' asked Bet.

The old woman looked suspicious. 'What are you spierin' for? What's it to you?'

'Oh, I was thinking that whoever it is will be hard put to find a tenant as good as you,' Bet flattered. 'Would that be Mr McKelvie?'

'It's Mr McAllister. He's got a grand office in the High Street, with his shiny plate on the front and all. Many a time he's said to me, "If they were all as good tenants as you, Mrs Barclay, I'd have no bother at all."

'Mind you, I've been at him to do this place up. "You'll be wanting electric light next, Mrs Barclay," he says to me. The impudence of it! "No," I says, very dignified, "I'm not asking for electric light. But it could do with a lick of paint." Still, I'll not be troubled, I'm out at the term.' She lapsed into a grumpy silence.

'How much?' asked Bet. 'For the taffy twist.'

'That'll be a ha'penny.'

The old woman took the coin and put it into the tin cash box.

The door bell clanged as the two girls made their way outside.

'What was all that about?' asked Alice. 'Why so many questions?'

'I wanted to know the name of the lawyer who lets this building,' said Bet firmly, turning back along the way they had come.

'Where are you off to? You're going the wrong way,' Alice called.

'No, I'm not,' said Bet. 'I'm on my way to see this Mr McAllister. It shouldn't be difficult to find where he is. Are you coming?'

'But...' Alice struggled to keep up with her friend, who was walking quickly along the way they had come. 'I still don't see...'

Bet stopped and turned to Alice with exasperation. 'You're being real stupid,' she said. 'Can you not see? The shop's going to close. The lawyer needs a tenant. Someone who'll brighten the place up, paint it, keep it clean and tidy, make customers stop and buy their sweeties there. There's not a sweetie shop for the next two or three streets, so we – you'd have the trade all to yourself. It could be a wee gold mine.'

'So...' Alice's face cleared. 'You think you and Jackie could run it?'

Bet beamed at her. 'Why not? Mind you, I'd have to persuade Jackie, and that might take a wee while, but first, I've to see this lawyer.'

As they made their way back to the High Street, Alice had a sudden thought.

'All that about looking at kid slippers and so on. I don't think you ever wanted to go and see the shops, did you? It was all an excuse.'

'Of course it was,' said Bet briskly. 'And I don't really like taffy twist either, but it was the only thing I could think of! Now, come on. We don't want to find he's closed for the day.'

They found the smart brass plaque announcing the offices of Mr McAllister. The door was open.

'Right,' said Bet, 'here we go.'

Chapter Ten

A Glow In Her Heart

Sundays were a bit drab, thought Alice. Everyone seemed to have a beau – everyone except her. There was the young man, Alec, who she had met at the Jameses' party. Once

188

or twice he had called for her and they'd gone for a walk in the park, but although he was genial company, she felt that friendship was enough, there would be nothing more. There were several lads at the works, one especially in the firing shed, who waited for her as she left after work one day.

'Can I walk you home, Miss?' he said hopefully. 'It's Tommy – you know me, I carry the pots to the lasses.'

'All right,' she said, and Tommy beamed and fell into step, striding along beside her.

'My, you can fair walk for a lassie,' he said. 'I've seen you with Bet – she's a character and no mistake.'

Alice was silent. She didn't want to snub him, but she had no wish to talk about Bet.

Earlier in the day, Bet had come up to her. 'I'll maybe have some good news soon,' she'd murmured with a wee smile.

Oh, why, thought Alice, in a burst of self-pity, did everyone have good news but her? And here was this nice, honest lad who would willingly have taken her to a dance, and she had nothing much to say to him.

She tried to make conversation but it was hard going. Tommy simply said, 'Aye,' or, 'That's right,' and gazed at her with an air of admiration.

'You're kind of different from the other lasses,' he said suddenly. 'You're more refined.'

'I'm just the same as them,' said Alice sharply. Why did everyone try to make out that she was better, cleverer, than the rest, just because she had a better job? She hated to discourage Tommy, but she didn't want to be put on a pedestal. And yet, was she being a snob? She didn't want to think so.

'Where do you stay?'

'Down Coal Row.'

'That's where young Eck bides – Chrissie's lad – isn't it?'

'I stay with Chrissie,' said Alice.

He shook his head. 'Then you'd best have a word with her about him.'

'Why?' Alice was concerned.

'He's in bad company. There was two or three of them broke into a house – two of them got nabbed by the police, but young Eck got away.'

Alice was shocked. 'How do you know?'

'The lads at the works were talking about it. They reckon young Eck was lucky to get away else he'd have been up in court with the others.'

'But he's only, what – not fourteen?'

'He'd not be sent to prison,' said Tommy.

'Just to a reform school. Mind you, it's maybe a bit late for young Eck to be reformed.'

'Chrissie never said anything.'

'Maybe she doesn't know. But you'd better warn her.'

'Thank you, Tommy.' She gave him a warm smile. 'You've done a good turn.'

'Me? I never did anything. But see, Miss, would you like to come with me to the dancing, maybe on Saturday?'

But Alice was already stepping into the close. 'Thanks for seeing me home,' she called over her shoulder, and vanished up the stairs, leaving Tommy standing looking after her. Then he shrugged and walked back the way he had come.

For a few days Alice thought about what he had said. She had noticed that Eck was often surly and silent, and would disappear for hours without saying where he was going. She knew how concerned Chrissie was, and yet, she didn't like to interfere...

She pushed these thoughts to the back of her mind. It was a specially busy time at the pottery, and she often had to work late to finish a tea set that was wanted for a wedding gift. More and more she was being given special commissions to decorate, perhaps a set of small boxes, or dressing-table sets.

So she was thinking about the decorating she had just completed as she returned home one evening, and though tired, she felt a sense of satisfaction. She knew she had done a good job, and Mr McCracken had nodded approvingly when he had come to inspect her work.

Her mind very much elsewhere, Alice stopped as she reached the door of her lodgings. She sniffed. That was strange – there was a strong smell of tobacco. And then she heard voices.

A little shyly, for she didn't know who Chrissie might be entertaining, she pushed open the door.

There at Chrissie's kitchen table sat a huge man with a ginger beard. He was wearing a shabby suit and a far-from-clean collar. He was drinking a cup of tea and had a scone halfway to his mouth.

When he saw Alice, he put the scone back on the plate.

'Hello,' said Alice hesitantly.

Chrissie turned from the stove, her face flushed and cheerful.

'Here you are,' she greeted Alice. 'This,' she said to the man at the table, 'is my lodger, Miss Finlay. And this–' she beamed proudly to Alice. 'This is my husband. This is Johnnie.'

Alice didn't know what to say.

'How do you do?' she managed at last.

The man rose from the table and shook her hand in a powerful grasp.

'Good to meet you, miss,' he said heartily.

'He's come back for good,' said Chrissie. 'And here was me thinking I'd not see him again.'

'I'm the bad penny that always turns up,' Johnnie chortled.

Alice was longing to know where he had been all this time, but she didn't like to ask. However, it wasn't long before Johnnie gave an account of his absence.

'I was round the world at sea. And I was away one winter with a whaler from Dundee – my, I'd not do that again.'

'Sit in and get your tea,' Chrissie told Alice.

Then Eck arrived. At first he, too, was silent, but after a bit he sat gazing in admiration at the huge bearded man he could hardly remember.

In the days that followed, the little house seemed crowded. Johnnie's vast presence seemed to fill the kitchen, and his roars of laughter could be heard through the walls till they reached Alice's small bedroom. She shut her ears, trying not to listen, and trying without success to concentrate on a book or a piece of sewing.

'You've had a very adventurous time,' she said one evening as they gathered round the table.

'I have that,' he replied. 'Would there be more tatties, Chrissie? Thank you kindly. I've fair missed your mince and tatties while I've been wayfaring. Though mind you, the cook on the voyage across the China Seas, he was a wonder. Except for shark fin soup – I never took to that.'

Since the return of his father, young Eck had stopped going out in the evenings. Instead he would sit and listen, rapt, to Johnnie's tales – about the time he had served on a whaler: 'A whole winter and we got stick in the ice', about his voyages round the Mediterranean; trips on a tramp steamer; and once, when he had had a great stroke of fortune, and was taken on as a deck hand on a luxury yacht.

'That's the life, I tell you – all those toffs drinking champagne, all day, starting in the morning.'

Alice had to admit that Johnnie was a good influence on his son. Once, when Eck cheeked Chrissie, he roared, 'Don't you speak to your mother like that or I'll take my belt to you, grown lad as you are.'

Eck subsided and after that didn't dare to give impudence to Chrissie.

As for Chrissie, she was like a girl again, blushing at some of Johnnie's remarks, putting her arms around him as she passed behind his chair, setting down the largest portion of food in front of her man.

'You need feeding up,' she said fondly.

'You might have written,' she said once. 'Not a scrape of the pen did I have all that time.'

'Och, Chris girl,' he said, 'you know I was never a great hand at writing. And besides, you canna read yourself.'

'I could have got someone to read it out to me,' she said.

'Not the kind of message I'd have been sending you,' he said slyly, making Chrissie blush again. Alice was pleased to see her landlady so patently happy to have her man back home.

'I'll need to see about getting a job,' said Johnnie from time to time. 'So's I can keep my wife and son in a proper style.'

'You're not going back to sea then?' asked Alice.

'No. I've had enough of the sea to last me the rest of my life. Until you've faced the Atlantic in a nor'-easter, you've no idea what hardship is.'

Certainly, thought Alice, mealtimes were much livelier now. Johnnie held the floor with tales of captains he had known, first mates who were crooked, or drunkards, or plain incompetent. There were tales of the tropics, of strange birds and beasts. There were stories of skulduggery, or magical sandy shores fringed with palm trees, or long hot tropical nights.

And certainly under his father's influence, Eck had improved in the space of a few weeks. Sometimes he would bring his friends in and they, too, would sit spellbound, listening to Johnnie's tales.

Chrissie, too. Her careworn look had gone, and she sparkled under Johnnie's affectionate teasing. Maybe he wasn't the brave young man who had led her in the Lancers, but he was her husband and home for good.

And his tales of the sea and strange foreign shores – Alice couldn't help being fascinated by Johnnie's account of his travels during the long past years. So why, she wondered, why didn't she believe a word of it?

'I'm away to take this lot of washing up to the Pottery House,' said Chrissie. 'I'll make you a cup of tea when I come back.'

'Take your time, lass,' Johnnie said, settling back in an armchair beside the fire and stretching out his hands to the blaze.

'Can I make the tea?' Alice offered.

'No, you sit there and have a blether with Johnnie. Eck'll be back soon.'

She bustled out leaving a silence behind her.

For the past few days, Alice, busy at work and tired out in the evening, had not seen much of Johnnie, though she was still aware of his large presence in the house.

'It's grand to be back at my own fireside, so it is,' he said now. 'After all these years of sailing round the world, the weather that hot you could have fried an egg on the sand. And the tropical storms – my, they were something! Did I ever tell you about the night we had to tie ourselves to the mast else we'd have been washed overboard?'

Suddenly Alice lost patience. 'Yes, you have – and I wish you'd be quiet about your so-called adventures.'

He looked astonished. '"So called"? Now, lass, that's no way to talk to a man that's sailed the seven seas and fought with wild

197

beasts and savages.'

'I wish you'd be quiet,' said Alice firmly, 'because I don't believe you.'

Johnnie was silent and Alice wondered if she had gone too far.

'Do you not?' he said, looking sideways at her. 'And why is that?'

'Well, for a start,' said Alice more boldly, 'if you'd been a sea-faring man as you say you were, then why are you so pale? You should have the face of a man who's been outdoors for years, like some of the fishermen along the coast. But you haven't. You don't look to me,' she said, 'as if you've been out of this country.'

'I was,' he protested, 'for a wee while.' He gave a chuckle. 'My, you're a bright one.'

'So where were you?'

'I was in the jail,' said Johnnie slowly. 'For some o' the time anyway.'

'I thought as much.'

'I got into bad company. A bit of house-breaking, that was how it began. And one thing led to another.'

'So what brought you back here?'

'When I got out of the jail – the last time, that was – I thought about going straight. I missed Chrissie. I'd had enough of sneaking around from one place to another. And I wanted to see my lad.' He paused. 'So what are you going to do about it, now you've guessed?'

'Me? It's nothing to do with me,' said Alice.

'You won't tell Chrissie?'

'Oh no. She's glad to have you back. I wouldn't spoil that for her.'

'Mind you–' he hesitated. '–sometimes she gives me a look, and I have the feeling that she knows more than she lets on. But the lad…'

'I won't say anything to him either,' Alice prompted. 'Unless–'

'Unless I go back to my old ways? No danger of that,' said Johnnie. 'I want to see that lad of mine growing up, learning a trade, not getting himself into the sort of life I had.'

'He's been getting into bad company already,' Alice warned him.

'I'll soon put a stop to that,' said Johnnie decisively. 'I want him to have a father he can look up to.'

He gazed into the fire then turned to Alice. 'So you'll keep quiet.'

'Of course.'

'Thanks. You're a pal. And you've been a friend to my Chrissie while I've been …

away.' He reached out and shook her hand. 'Thanks, Alice.'

'Well?' said Alice when she and Bet met a few days later. 'Go on, tell me all about it.'

She couldn't help noticing that Bet was like a different person. Her eyes were sparkling, her hair seemed to have a new sheen, and there was a new air of confidence about her.

'I went to see the lawyer, as you know,' Bet told her.

Alice nodded. 'And…?'

'And he said we can rent the shop. To be honest,' Bet added, 'it's in such a state that I don't think anyone else wants it. I think he was pleased that someone would take it over.'

'You said "we"?' Alice echoed hopefully.

'To begin with,' Bet confided, 'I had the feeling that Jackie thought it was a bit of a come-down, him serving sweeties instead of being a fisherman. But after a bit, he got to like the idea of doing up the shop, starting a business that would be our very own. And there's a room and kitchen over the shop.'

'So…?'

'So, we couldn't be living there in sin, could we?' Bet's dark eyes sparkled. 'So once he'd come round to the idea of renting the shop and us running it together, he said we'd have to get married. Only,' she added hastily, 'he didn't put it quite like that. A bit more romantic, you know.'

'Oh, Bet! I'm so pleased for you both,' said Alice, giving her friend a hug. 'I know you'll make a real go of it.'

'The room and kitchen...' Bet wrinkled her nose. 'It's a midden. How anyone could live that way, I don't know. But I'll soon get it cleaned up, and I'm going to make curtains and cushions, and my auntie's giving us two old chairs.'

'And when's the wedding to be?' Alice asked.

'We get the shop on the first of January, so we'll get wed on Hogmanay. You'll be my bridesmaid, won't you?'

'Of course I will,' said Alice.

'Mind you,' said Bet frankly, 'it won't be the wedding I'd planned. I won't be in a lacy veil and with a big bouquet of carnations and fern. I'll just wear my best dress, and maybe a new hat. And we won't have a big spread, just tea at our place, after the wedding at the manse.' She laughed. 'Me with all my grand plans for a big wedding, eh? But d'you know, it doesn't matter a docken to me, not as long as I've got Jackie.'

'Oh, I'm really glad,' said Alice. 'You deserve it, you both do.'

'There's just one wee problem,' said Bet, her face clouding. 'You know his mother's a widow? Jackie's the only one. And he's been bringing in a wage – well, up to a while ago, when he had the accident. It's not that so much – we can still manage to help her, but she'll be lonely in that wee place down by the harbour. Mind you, she's not one to stand in our way, but I'm kind of anxious for her.'

Alice paused, thinking what a good-hearted soul Bet was.

'I think the answer would be for her to take a lodger,' said Bet. 'Maybe a nice single man, or a woman coming in from work. Someone to cook for, cheer the place up a bit. She wouldn't be asking much in the way of rent, would she?'

Alice knew she was impulsive sometimes, but this seemed like a very good opportunity. She hesitated, but only for a moment.

'In fact, what about me? Would I do?'

'You?' Bet gazed at her friend in astonishment. 'But you're at Chrissie's. Is there something wrong there?'

'No, no,' said Alice hastily. 'But you know

202

her man's come home from – from his travels?'

'Do I not!' Bet laughed. 'Eck's full of it – all about his father being on the China Seas, and on a whaler – he's been telling my wee brother.'

'Well,' said Alice, 'not that they've said anything, but I feel maybe they'd like the place to themselves, now they're a family again.'

'Jackie's mother keeps a very clean house,' said Bet eagerly. 'And she's a grand baker – you should taste her soda scones.'

'Then could I come with you and see her?' Alice asked, smiling.

'Tomorrow night?' said Bet. 'Would that suit you?'

'Surely,' said Alice. 'So...' she added, 'this means you'll be putting in your notice at Simpson's.'

Bet nodded. 'I'll miss you, we've had some good laughs together. But you'll come and see us, won't you? Promise.'

'Of course I will,' said Alice. 'I wouldn't buy my barley sugars anywhere else!'

'Do you think it would suit you?' Jackie's mother asked anxiously. 'There's not a lot of space for your things.'

'I don't have a lot of things,' Alice reassured her. 'I just have a few clothes – and all I want is a little space for drawing and painting.'

'Bet said you're an artist,' said Mrs Keith, impressed. She blinked up at Alice a little short-sightedly and smoothed the front of her apron. 'I'm not used to young ladies,' she said, hesitating. 'They maybe like things dainty, and I'm just a plain cook. My Jackie liked hearty dinners.'

'Please don't worry, Mrs Keith, it'll be grand,' said Alice. This felt odd, almost as if it were she who were interviewing the older woman. 'And I'm not a real artist, just a beginner. That's just Bet exaggerating.'

'Oh, Bet,' said the woman, beaming. 'A fine lassie, and she'll make a good wife to my Jackie.'

Alice agreed, and as they went on to talk about terms, and washing and meals, she looked around the room approvingly. It was spotless, with a clean cotton bedspread, and freshly distempered walls. And best of all, the light was good. 'I can work here,' she thought.

The only remaining hurdle was that she had to tell Chrissie that she was leaving. She was dreading it. Might Chrissie think it was a slur on her housekeeping?

Alice tried, haltingly, to explain. 'It's not that I'm not happy here. You've made it so comfortable. But I know it's a bit crowded here – and you could use my room for Eck.

At first Chrissie was dismayed. 'I never thought,' she said.

'It's nothing to do with you,' Alice tried to reassure her. 'Just I maybe could do with space for painting – and you need the space, too. And now that Johnnie's working...' For Johnnie had at last bestirred himself and had been taken on at the linoleum works.

'It's a far cry from the open seas,' he said in his booming voice, then he caught Alice's eye and fell silent.

'Aye, I've been glad of the money,' Chrissie admitted. 'But now...'

'And,' Alice went on, 'it means that Jackie and Bet can get married and move to the shop without him worrying that his mother will be left alone.'

That seemed to settle the matter for Chrissie. Her romantic soul had thrilled to the story of Bet's love affair. She had been saddened when it had seemed it was all over, and delighted when Alice had told her the wedding was to go ahead after all.

'I'll miss you,' she said. 'You've been a

grand lodger.'

'I'll not be far away,' said Alice, 'and I'll come and see you.'

'You make sure you do.'

Once Alice had moved to her new lodgings, she decided it was time to work even harder at her painting. She knew she was learning a lot about decorating, thanks to Miss Gray. And Mr James was an excellent tutor, always demanding, but encouraging, too. And there was the practical help he gave, without being at all patronising.

'Tsk,' he said one day, 'these brushes I ordered, they're not at all what I wanted. And I've tried them out – I can't send them back. I'll just need to throw them out. Unless–' he paused '–would they be any use to you? They're not top quality, mind.'

Alice looked at the brushes, and wondered if he was being quite honest. She could see nothing wrong with them.

'Yes, please,' she said eagerly.

Then there was the paper.

'For goodness' sake, girl,' he said, 'don't go wasting your money on paper – there's stacks of it here I won't use. Help yourself.'

Or there might be a few jars of paint, already opened.

'It's a pity to throw these away – are they any use to you?'

Alice tried to thank him, but he waved her away.

'You go on painting, girl,' he said. 'Go on improving, that's the way to thank me.'

From time to time, Mr James and Rebecca gave evening parties. Alice hoped very much that she would meet again the tall dark man who had chatted to her at that first soirée. She could remember his voice, the way he had looked at her.

'But he was only being polite,' she thought.

Still, it intrigued her. Who was he? Rebecca clearly could not remember. She decided to ask Mr James – *very* casually.

As she dipped her brush in water and concentrated on the shades of a grey-green leaf, she said in an odd-hand way, 'You and Mrs James – Rebecca – you know a lot of artists, don't you?'

'A few,' he said. 'There's a lot of interesting work being done. You've heard of some of the new people – Fergusson, Cadell?'

Alice shook her head.

He went on. 'Fergusson, for example. Quite different from anything we've seen – vibrant colours, striking scenes, a lot of pictures of the South of France. You can feel the warmth of the sun. Cadell, too – he's one of the new boys. It's exciting, what they're doing.' He ran his fingers through his hair.

'Tell you what,' he said. 'Next time there's an exhibition on in Edinburgh or maybe Glasgow, come with us. It'll open your eyes, I promise you.'

'I'd really like to. Thank you,' said Alice. She added casually, 'That evening party you and Rebecca gave – there was a painter there.'

'Lots of painters there,' he said. 'Rebecca likes to fill the house.'

'Tall, well-dressed, dark,' Alice pressed on. 'He was interesting, the way he talked.'

'Well-dressed, eh?' He gave a laugh. 'Couldn't have been anyone we knew. They're an untidy, bedraggled lot, the painters we know. No money to speak of. I can't think who he might have been – not one of our friends anyway. But you'll meet some more of them, that's for sure. One or two gifted, more of them just amateurs.

'Well, now, let's get on with the work... Have you looked at that leaf? Haven't you noticed the difference in greens?' He shook his head. 'Haven't I taught you anything?'

'Forget him,' Alice told herself later that

day. 'You were just someone to chat to – why should he remember you? Stop dreaming, girl, and think about your work.'

Mr James had given her exercises.

'It's time you learned to look at buildings,' he said. 'We'll start on those next week.'

She was determined to learn all she could and achieve her ambition.

'Some day I *will* be an artist.'

But all the same, she gave a little sigh. Everyone needed a little romance in their lives, didn't they? And it didn't look, thought Alice, as if there was going to be any in hers.

However, she was greatly cheered one evening when, hurrying across the yard, at the works she bumped into a young man who looked vaguely familiar.

'Steady on.' He held her arm and smiled at her. 'You're in a hurry.'

It was Mr Henry, the overseer's son.

'I know you,' he said. 'You're the artist, aren't you?'

'Well...' Alice hesitated.

'Don't be so modest.' He grinned. 'I've heard about you. And I've seen your work. It was you, wasn't it, who did that sketch of my father?'

Alice blushed and stammered. 'I didn't mean...'

'Oh, he brought it home and showed it to us, tickled pink, he was. Said the lassie had got him off to a T. Not that he'd mention it to you, but he was real pleased. He said no one had ever done a drawing of him before.'

'I'm glad,' Alice hesitated. 'I thought he might be offended.'

'Not a bit of it.' The young man beamed at her. 'Keep on at your drawing, miss.' And he was off, raising his hat to her.

Alice gazed after him. Despite his good looks, he was not quite the young man of her dreams. But for all that, no knight in shining armour could, just then, have brought such a glow to her heart.

Chapter Eleven

A Good New Year

'My, but you're strangers!' Leaving work one evening, Bet and Alice stopped at the sight of the neatly dressed young woman waiting for them.

'Nannie! I hardly recognised you!' Alice greeted her. It was some time since she'd seen Nannie, and she felt a little guilty that she hadn't called round at the house.

'Well,' Nannie blushed. 'I'm earning a good wage now. She's that kind, Miss Todd – and she raised my pay just a month back. And she let me make a new skirt for myself.' She beamed at them. 'I'm real lucky.'

'And your mother?' Alice hardly liked to ask.

'I pay a woman to go in and see to her while I'm at work.' Nannie gave a little laugh. 'She doesn't stand any nonsense – makes my mother do a bit of cleaning, and get a meal most nights…'

Alice, remembering the slatternly woman who was Nannie's mother, could hardly believe it.

'I heard you're to be married,' said Nannie to Bet, 'and I just wanted to wish you well. And this–' she handed a packet to Bet '–is a wee minding. I hope you and your lad will be happy.'

'Oh!' Bet was quite overcome. She untied the blue ribbon that bound the packet and gazed in admiration at the exquisitely worked lace handkerchiefs. 'They're beautiful! That was real kind of you. Thank you.'

'I thought you'd like one to carry with you at your wedding,' said Nannie.

'Something new and something blue,' said Alice. 'Now all you need is something old and something borrowed…'

'I'll find those all right.' Bet was smiling again after wiping away a tear. 'Listen, Nannie – it's just a small wedding – you maybe heard about Jackie being injured. But would you like to come?'

'Really? Oh, I would that.' Nannie beamed. 'It will be a pleasure.'

'It's on Hogmanay,' said Bet. 'With the reception at my mother's place. That sounds grand, doesn't it? A reception. But it'll be a good evening, and I'd really like you to come.'

Nannie's rosy face became even rosier with delight. 'I wouldn't miss it for anything.'

After that the days seemed to pass even more quickly. The shop windows showed Christmas and Ne-er Day gifts, and people began to look forward to the year 1910.

Bet's wedding on Hogmanay may have been a lot quieter than the one she had planned, but the guests remembered it as a happy and joyous occasion. It began with the 'poor-out'. Bet insisted that they followed the old traditions, so when the groom and best man left his home for the ceremony, they threw small coins – a few halfpence, some farthings – to the crowd of urchins that scrambled around the two men, shouting, 'Poor-out, poor-out.'

The ceremony itself was held in the manse parlour. In her best dress of navy serge with a high collar and pin-tucked bodice, Bet looked smart. Alice knew how she had longed for a proper bouquet and had suggested to the girls at the pottery that they club together and buy a few flowers, so Bet carried a spray of hothouse carnations and fern – perhaps not as grand as the one she had dreamt of, but a wedding bouquet all the same.

Alice, standing behind her, was a witness, and Jackie's friend Bob had come as the other witness.

It was a short, very simple ceremony, but Alice, catching sight of Bet's face as she looked up at Jackie, had no doubt what it meant to her friend. Seeing Bet aglow with happiness, she felt a lump come in to her throat.

Afterward, there was a happy gathering at Bet's home. Her mother, who looked like an older version of Bet, rushed backwards and forwards with plates and glasses. There was a steak pie and trifle, and everyone enjoyed the feast.

Finally Bob, his brow perspiring in the heat of the parlour, called for silence.

'Have you all got a glass of ginger?' he asked. 'Then here's a toast. To the happy couple – long life and all the best.'

Everyone raised their glasses of ginger beer. 'To Bet and Jackie!' 'To the happy couple!'

Alice looked round the guests crammed into the parlour. There was Nannie, trim in a dark red woollen dress.

'I made it myself,' she'd told Alice, and then added, 'Isn't this a grand wedding? And look, she's carrying the handkerchief I made.'

There were others from the works. Mr McCracken had sent his good wishes and, to Bet's astonishment, a set of teaspoons from himself and his wife.

'Fancy that,' she'd said to Alice. 'I never knew he had a heart.'

One of Jackie's brothers had brought his accordion, and soon people started singing, and asking for favourite songs, until Jackie called for silence.

'It's just a few minutes to go,' he said, 'till the New Year.'

There was a stir as Bob was chosen as the first foot. 'Tall, dark and handsome,' said

Bet approvingly.

He was sent out of the house, clutching a piece of black bun and lump of coal, to hang about on the landing until the stroke of midnight, and the dawning of 1910.

'Fancy that,' said one of the elderly aunts. 'I wonder what it'll bring us?' And she sighed as if she were not quite sure what would happen.

'Cheer up, Auntie,' said Bet's father, pulling on his long whiskers. 'We've begun with a wedding – you can't get much better than that.'

And then the clock chimed twelve and Bob knocked loudly on the door.

'Come away in, come in,' cried Bet's mother.

'A good New Year to one and all,' said Bob, giving her a hearty kiss. And then he kissed one of the elderly aunts, who hadn't been kissed by a young man for years and years and thought the New Year hadn't begun too badly after all! And then he kissed Bet, and told her she was a lucky girl to have found someone like Jackie.

'It's me that's the lucky one,' said Jackie, giving his new wife a resounding kiss.

Someone started playing the accordion again and everyone joined in the singing and the toasts.

'A good New Year to one and all!' 'A good New Year!'

'It's lovely.' Alice looked with admiration round the little room. Bet had made it bright and welcoming, even though it had been done on a shoestring. The curtains were made of ticking, and she had added bright cushions made from remnants. A fire burned cheerfully in the grate, and on the mantelpiece were one or two pieces of pottery – a china hen, a mug which proclaimed itself a present from Rothesay – and one or two bits of brassware, polished until you could see your face in them.

'You *have* worked hard,' said Alice, and Bet beamed proudly.

'I've enjoyed it, making a home for us.'

'You don't miss the pottery?'

'Me? No. Old Frosty and Jess and – well, the girls were all right. But it was hard work, and tiring. This is hard work, too, but it's for us – for Jackie and me.'

Alice felt a little twinge of envy, but then she told herself firmly, 'You've got much more than Bet has ever had. And look what she's done, when it seemed at one time as if she had no rosy future at all.'

216

'This is for you,' said Bet shyly. 'Thank you for helping us.'

'But I didn't do anything!' Alice protested.

'Yes, you did. You came with me to look at the shop. I might not have had the nerve myself.'

'You – scared? I don't believe it,' Alice laughed. 'Bet, oh, Bet, you shouldn't have...' She looked at the beautiful box of chocolates tied with a pink ribbon. 'I'll treasure this.'

'Don't treasure them, just eat them,' said Bet briskly, and the two girls laughed together.

A few days later, Alice called to see her old teacher Miss Lennox.

'Well, I thought you'd forgotten me,' the woman said in a stern tone.

'I hadn't– I'm sorry, I meant to...' Alice was flustered, not realising she was being teased.

'Don't be ridiculous, girl, I don't take offence. Come through to the parlour and tell me what you've been up to.'

Later, sitting over a cup of tea and freshly baked scones, Miss Lennox said, 'I hear you're doing well with Mr James.'

'How...?'

'Oh, I know lots of people.' Miss Lennox

stretched out a thin hand towards the teapot. 'Another cup?'

She went on, 'I see them sometimes at a discussion group. The talk often turns to Fred's pupils. And he says you're his star student.'

Alice blushed. 'Me?'

'He doesn't praise lightly,' said Miss Lennox, 'so if you're doing well by his standards, you're doing very well indeed.'

'Oh!' Alice's face shone, and her old teacher thought how this girl had changed from the thin, pathetic little orphan she had first known. Now this tall slim girl with her shining hair and fresh open complexion looked confident and relaxed.

'So tell me about the pottery. How's your work going there?'

'It gets a bit dull at times,' Alice confessed, 'even though I always wanted to be a decorator. But then, when I've finished a piece I look at it, and think – well, that it's going to someone maybe as a gift, to stand on a dressing table, to be treasured in the family, and that makes it better.'

'Hm... And your friend Bet is no longer there?'

'No, but you should see how nice she's made their rooms. And the shop – well, they've cleaned it up, and it all looks so bright and appealing. People stop and look in the window now. And Jackie – he's a different person.

'They're getting to know everyone in the district. Little children come in to spend maybe a ha'penny; a lad will come in for conversation lozenges and old folk for their pan drops. And Jackie's so cheery. He jokes with people and the old folk come in and tell him their worries. I know he goes round and does repairs for some of them.'

'Good,' said Miss Lennox. 'By the way, I'm currently giving away some of my things – could they use a sofa, do you think? It's not new, but it's in good condition.'

'They'd be really pleased,' said Alice. 'I'll tell Jackie to call round.'

'There are some other things I'm disposing of,' said Miss Lennox, not looking at Alice. 'I'd like you to have this ring–' She produced a little velvet box from a drawer in a side table and passed it to Alice.

Alice opened it to find a beautiful ring set with garnets and diamonds.

'But I can't take this!' she stammered.

'Of course you can, I'm giving it to you,' said Miss Lennox briskly. 'And maybe what would be more use to you, too. You see, I don't need my money. And rather than leaving it you in my will, I'd like you to have it now. I thought maybe you'd like to train at art school. It would help with the fees.'

'But...' Alice didn't know what to say.

'If Fred James thinks you're good enough, that's a recommendation in itself. Anyway,' she continued, 'there's no getting away from the fact that I'm getting old, and I don't want my nephews and cousins – a greedy bunch – squabbling over my money after I've gone. I'd rather give it away now to whoever *I* choose. My,' she chuckled, 'won't they get a surprise when they find there's so little left for them?

'So,' she said, 'I'm giving it to you now.' She rose stiffly and went to her desk.

'Here you are.' She handed Alice a cheque.

Alice couldn't think what to say.

'But ... it's so good of you... I can't ever thank you enough.'

'You can thank me by working hard, making a real success of your life.' She looked out of the window and Alice noticed not for the first time how drawn and thin she looked these days.

'You're a good girl, Alice. I feel about you as if you were my own daughter and–' her voice broke '–I wish you were.'

'You're not trying,' said Mr James sternly. 'I want to see something original. Use your imagination, girl.'

'But I thought...' Alice bit her lip and looked at the scene she had painted of the sand dunes, looking towards the old town.

Mr James's voice was calmer now. 'Don't just look at a scene with another painter's eyes. But at the same time remember what I've told you – look at the pictures of Fergusson, Cadell, Peploe. Look at their techniques, how they use light and shade, their use of colour. Then go away and paint your own picture. You see?'

Alice nodded and he looked satisfied.

'All right. See you next week at the same time.'

'And how is your most promising student?' Rebecca appeared at the door as Alice made ready to leave. 'My dear, you must be exhausted,' she said to her. 'Come through to the kitchen and have some lemonade.'

Alice gratefully sank down on the wooden settle, admiring the colourful jars and jugs on the old dresser. Blue and white, pewter, lustre jugs... Suddenly she had an idea.

'Rebecca, would you mind if I borrowed one of your jugs?'

'Of course not. Take whatever you like.'

Alice selected a lustre jug. 'I'll take great care of it, I promise.'

'For a picture?' said Rebecca. 'Then take some of my roses, too. They're just at their best.'

Rebecca poured out the lemonade and Alice drank it gratefully, then she went out to the garden to gather one or two deep pink cabbage roses, and to cut a few of the small white roses on a bush by the gate.

'The truly Scots rose,' said Rebecca, who had followed her out. 'A very old one. That one goes back to Jacobite times. Imagine!'

Alice's mind conjured up a picture of Bonnie Prince Charlie and his followers. Maybe they had picked the rose, small, white, thorny, as it grew by the wayside.

At home, she set up her table by the window and placed the white rose in a jam jar. It didn't look right, somehow. So she tried it in the little jug she'd borrowed. Not enough. She laid the second white rose in front of the jug, as if someone had carelessly left it out of the picture.

'That's more like it.' She looked approvingly at the composition, picked up her pencil, and began sketching quickly.

'I like this,' said Mr James, standing in front of Alice's picture. 'It's got depth. You've caught the light on the leaves – the sunlight coming through the window and the white against the black jug. Yes, it's a good piece of work. You've come on a lot.'

This was real praise, thought Alice. But she was even more surprised when Mr James continued, 'Is it all right if I keep it? I like to have my pupils' work on show.'

'Of course.' Alice was astonished. 'Is it really good enough?'

'It's not bad.' Frederick James chuckled. 'I'll put it up here.' He placed it on a shelf. 'That will do for now. I've probably got a frame somewhere. A narrow black frame that would set it off well. And now, back to work...'

Every week when she went for her lesson, Alice looked at the picture. Mr James had yet to frame it. She was studying the work of modern Scots painters now, looking at their techniques, learning all the time, as Mr James had advised her.

'I'll never be good enough,' she sometimes told herself crossly, and would fling down her brush in despair.

Oh, she thought, why was life so drab, all of a sudden? There was Bet happily married, settled in the rooms above the shop with her Jackie.

There was Nannie, who had confided in Alice the other week, 'I've got a lad.'

'Have you really?' Alice had given her a warm hug. 'That's wonderful news.'

'We're walking out,' Nannie had gone on. 'And – well, it's serious.'

'I'm so pleased for you. Where did you meet him?'

'At a social at the church.' Nannie was longing to tell all the details. 'He's in the linoleum works, earning a good pay now.' She blushed. 'I'll maybe be making my own wedding dress before long.'

And even Jess – poor Jess, thought Alice, with all her bragging about a grand wedding and a show of presents. A few weeks ago, she had come across her standing outside the shed.

'Are you all right?'

'I'm just a wee bit faint. I'm aye like this in the mornings.'

Alice had been surprised. Surely not...?

'Aye, I'm having a bairn.' Jess had shrugged.

'Is he–' Alice hadn't known what to say.

'Oh, aye, it's Dougie. We've been courting a long time, and he'll wed me anyway.' She'd put a hand to her stomach. 'Afore it gets to showing.'

'Are you … pleased?' Alice had stumbled.

'Well, I'll be glad when it's here. Dougie wants a laddie,' she'd said with something of her old boastful spirit.

'What did your mother say?'

'She gave me a raging,' Jess had said frankly. 'But, och, she's fine about it now. What's one more grandchild to her, when she's got eight already? But she said we can just go up to the manse and get married quietly, and she'll tell the neighbours the bairn was a bit early. They'll not believe her, mind,' she added a little gloomily. 'And we'll have to live with Dougie's folks to begin with.' She'd looked sideways at Alice. 'I've not seen you with a lad lately. Are you not courting?'

Alice had shaken her head. Still, she'd thought, as she went back to work, it would be fine to have a lad.

There was something missing from the studio. Alice just couldn't think what it was. Mr James was standing by the window, cleaning his brushes, smiling. Finally she realised what it was.

'Where's my picture?' she asked suddenly.

'It's being framed,' he said. 'You have your first sale.'

'But … but…' Alice stammered. 'But how … who?'

He smiled at her. 'I sometimes sell work – my own, Rebecca's, work by an exceptionally talented pupil – and the buyer just happened to be looking for something with a Scottish feel to it for a special gift. Your Scots roses seemed to fit the bill.'

'What … I mean…' she stammered, overwhelmed by the news.

Mr James chuckled. 'You want to know how much I sold it for, don't you? By rights I should be charging you commission.'

'Oh, I didn't mean that.' Alice blushed. 'I don't really want the money – you deserve it more than me.'

'Oh, Alice, you will never make a businesswoman. If you are going to be an artist, you must learn to value your work. Don't give it away. But never mind – I'll get you a cheque, or I can pay it into your post office account. Would that be better?'

'Thank you.' Alice felt her head spinning.

'Now,' said Frederick James, 'we must get down to work. Don't let this first sale go to your head.'

But Alice found it hard to concentrate that

day. As she walked homeward, she kept saying to herself, 'I am an artist, a real artist! I have sold a painting. And there will be others.'

It was some weeks later. Alice had arrived early that Saturday afternoon at the Jameses' and was pinning a piece of paper to her board. From time to time she glanced at her rose painting which had now been framed, the narrow black wood setting off the white roses and the glowing texture of the vase. She wondered a little about the buyer; if it was for a gift, she hoped it would be a pleasant surprise.

Mr James had been setting up a still life – some red-skinned apples, a mug with a pattern of cherries, a plain circular table, highly polished. The doorbell rang, and he glanced up.

'I'd better go and see who it is ... Rebecca's out.'

Alice, preoccupied with her work, heard his voice greet the visitor.

'Come in, come in. You're here to collect the picture? It's all ready for you. It's been framed. I think you'll be pleased with it. And–' He opened the door of the studio with a flourish '–you're in luck because you can meet the artist.'

Alice rose as the two men entered the room. Standing against the light, her auburn hair swept up in an untidy knot, she was conscious of her paint-splattered smock, a dab of blue paint on her cheek. For a moment, she could not quite take in what she was seeing.

'So you are the artist?' the visitor exclaimed. 'I had no idea.'

'May I introduce Mr Angus Gilmour – Miss Alice Finlay,' said Frederick James.

'We have met once before, at the soirée,' the younger man said, smiling broadly at Alice. 'And you are the painter of this charming picture?'

'Well, I never,' said Frederick, looking from one to the other. 'Imagine that.'

'You never told me,' said Angus Gilmour, a little reproachfully, 'that this particular pupil was the artist.'

'Well, now,' said Frederick, pleased. 'I'm glad the picture you chose was Alice's. She is, though I don't often tell her so, hardworking and talented, and I think she has a future.'

Alice went pink, uncertain of how to reply.

'Now we will get the picture packed up, ready to present to your mother,' Frederick said briskly. 'And then I'll make us a cup of tea since Rebecca isn't here today. Brown paper, string – now where are they? Excuse me a moment, please.'

Left alone with Alice, Angus said, 'I remember how we talked that evening. I haven't been back in Scotland until recently – our family business has taken me to the Baltic. Do you perhaps remember our conversation?'

'Oh, yes,' said Alice. 'But I thought – I thought you were an artist, perhaps one of Rebecca's friends. You seemed to know a great deal about paintings.'

He laughed. 'No, I'm not an artist, I'm in our family's shipping business. But I'm interested in art, in collecting pictures. And yours – if I may say so – has a freshness about it. It's just what I wanted for my mother's present, for a special birthday.'

'I hope she likes it.' Alice smiled at him.

'I must tell you before Frederick returns, that I don't think I've ever spent a more enjoyable evening – talking to you, I mean. I've thought about it often. I hoped that perhaps we might meet again.' He hesitated. 'Of course, you must meet a great many people, but I hoped that perhaps you might remember our meeting, our conversation.'

Alice considered saying airily, 'Not really,' or, 'Well, vaguely,' but looking into the dark eyes and the face that was smiling at her, she said suddenly and quite impulsively, 'Oh, yes, oh, yes!'

And that is why, when Frederick returned with brown paper and a knotted tangle of string, the buyer of the picture was holding the artist's hand, and they were looking at each other with astonishment.

'Dear me,' he said to himself. 'Well, well. What a very surprising thing. Wait till I tell Rebecca…'

Chapter Twelve

Years Go By, Bringing New Generations

'I don't care what Dad says,' Karen yelled back, and Jo looked despairingly at her younger daughter. Why did there have to be such strife between Karen and her father? If it wasn't Karen's orange spikey hair, or her T-shirts with slogans, it was coming in late, or lying in bed till mid-morning.

But these were normal parent/teenager rows. This latest one was more serious. Karen was determined to go to art school.

Teaching art, now that Bob could understand. But she was good with computers – why not do an IT course?

But Karen wouldn't be swayed. She had set her heart on art school.

'The teachers say I'm good enough,' she insisted. And Jo, looking at her daughter's portfolio, agreed. Karen certainly had talent.

'But you know it's not enough to have talent. There are hundreds out there with as much talent as you. You have to work really hard.'

'I'm not scared of hard work.' Karen assumed the determined expression that Jo recognised from her childhood.

'I'll talk to your father,' Jo promised.

'They don't want me to go to art college,' Karen told her grandmother.

'By "they", I presume you mean your parents?'

Karen nodded. 'Dad wants me to do something with computers. Well, computers are OK, but I want to be an artist. And Mum doesn't say much but she isn't actually encouraging. I think they see me as starving in a garret. It's ridiculous! There's more to life,' said Karen loftily, 'than making a lot of money. I'm good enough to go to art school, I know I am. My teachers say so. But – oh, there's never been an artist in our family…'

'Oh, yes there was.' Laura interrupted Karen's flow of words. 'Way back. Your great-great-grandmother? Yes, I think that's right.'

'Who was she? And why haven't I heard about her?'

'Well, according to my mother – that's your great-grandmother – she died some time in the Fifties. I never knew her, but she sounded a fascinating person.'

'I can't believe she's just been forgotten.'

Laura shook her head. 'People weren't that interested in family history, not until recently. I've started going to a class on researching your family history through the internet.' Laura's eyes gleamed. 'It's wonderful what you can learn. We're going to find our family history from maps and military records, and records of emigrants – you can trace people who went to Canada, way back.'

'So would you be able to find out about Great-great-grandmother?'

'Certainly. I'll have a go at least.'

A week later, Laura proudly produced a

family tree.

'Here we are – my detective work.' She spread it out on the table. 'There's the family. You and your brothers ... me ... *my* mother – she was your great-grandmother. She was born around 1917. And back to Alice Gilmour – she was your great-great-grandmother.'

'Born 1890,' said Karen thoughtfully. 'And *her* parents, James and Alexandra – oh, they died when she was only five years old. What a shame! What happened to them?'

'The father was lost at sea, I believe. And Alice's mother, well, it could have been typhoid,' Laura said sombrely. 'It often was in those days.'

'So what would have happened to Alice?'

'If there weren't any relatives, she probably went into an orphanage.'

'Poor little girl,' Karen sighed.

'My mother knew a little bit about her,' said Laura. 'She worked in a pottery, then had drawing lessons, and then, with the help of a legacy, she went to art school.'

'Goodness,' said Karen. 'That was quite an achievement for an orphan.'

'She was very determined, my mother said. Even as an old lady. Mother said she became quite well known in her day – not in the top league like Phoebe Traquair and women artists like her, but all the same...'

'And who did she marry?'

'Someone called Angus Gilmour. It was quite romantic, I gather, the way they met, though I never heard the full story.'

'Here he is...' Karen looked at the family tree. 'Oh, died 1917.'

'Yes, he was killed in the First World War. So many were. Your great-grandmother never knew her father.'

'I wish,' said Karen thoughtfully, 'that I knew more about her. A real artist in the family, and no-one much interested. What a shame.'

'Maybe,' said Laura, 'I could find out where her paintings are. They're probably in someone's attic. They won't be valuable, I shouldn't think – just of family interest.'

A few weeks later, Laura came back in triumph. 'Guess what! I've tracked down a painting by Alice. It's in a gallery in Perthshire, in their local history collection.'

'How did you find it? What sort of painting?'

'Through the internet,' said Laura modestly. 'It's amazing what you can find.'

'You silver surfers,' Karen teased. 'Well, are we going to see it?'

'How about next Saturday?'

Karen couldn't believe she was so excited about going to see a painting by someone who was only a distant member of the family, but somehow Alice's story had caught her imagination.

'I wish I'd asked my mother more about her,' said Laura, as they drove along. 'But you don't think, at the time. And I wish, too, that I had some of the pottery she decorated.'

'Was it like Wemyss ware?'

'Not as well known. But at Simpson's – that was the pottery she worked for – they painted flowers and fruit. Most potteries did in those days. Mugs for special occasions, plates, dressing-table sets.'

They turned into the town square and parked the car. Inside the library they were shown the way to the local history section.

'Alice Finlay?' said the girl behind the desk. 'Yes, we have one of her paintings. She lived round here, I gather. In the 1920s.'

'Can we see the picture?' Karen was eager with excitement.

'It's on the far wall. An oil. Still life with roses.'

Karen and Laura stood silently before the picture. A delicate spray of an old-fashioned white rose in a black lacquered vase set on a highly polished table. Another rose lay in the foreground. The artist had captured the texture of the bloom and the soft green of the leaves, and the whole picture seemed to glow with life.

Karen said, in a whisper, 'It's beautiful.'

Laura nodded. 'She was talented. It's a shame she wasn't better known.'

Karen turned to the librarian. 'Do you know anything about her?'

The girl shook her head. 'Not a lot. She lived around here. Painted poppies, wild flowers, farmyard scenes. Sometimes they come up at auction but they don't fetch a lot. Out of fashion, I'm afraid. But you never know when the fashions will change. You know about her?'

'She was my great-great-grandmother,' said Karen with some pride.

'That's wonderful.' The girl smiled. 'You must be very proud of her.'

'Oh, I am,' said Karen. 'I am.'

'To think,' said Karen later, 'that I never knew about her. Yet it's such a fascinating story – the orphan and her struggle to be an artist.'

Laura agreed. 'Don't forget that was about a hundred years ago. People today don't have the same kind of struggle. If there's talent there, you can get grants, and bursaries, and there's much more opportunity.'

'No,' said Karen. 'It's a different kind of struggle, maybe. Now I have to persuade Dad that he needs an artist in the family – another artist. I won't let you down,' she said softly.

'Me?' Laura was surprised.

'No.' Karen smiled. 'Not you, Gran. Alice. I won't let her down. I promise.'

The publishers hope that this book has given you enjoyable reading. Large Print Books are especially designed to be as easy to see and hold as possible. If you wish a complete list of our books please ask at your local library or write directly to:

Dales Large Print Books
Magna House, Long Preston,
Skipton, North Yorkshire.
BD23 4ND